AF446116

Luna Blackwood wishes to aknowledge the traditional custodians of the

land on which this story was written, the Whadjuk Noongar people.

Special thanks to Max Vos

Chloe sat on the old leather couch of the locker room, lacing up her boots. She was having more trouble than usual today, her vision blurred as she held back tears, her hands shaking as she pulled at the laces. Sighing heavily in frustration, she realised she hadn't eaten since the pervious morning. Dropping her head into her hands, she pushed her palms against her eyes in a vain effort to hold her tears in. Frustrated, she scolded herself quietly, "Hold it together, Chloe. You're a professional." She turned her attention to the side table, covered in a pile of months old magazines. She'd made it halfway through the work day, but it was getting harder and harder to fake being fine. Thankfully at this time of day, nobody else was in the locker room, and nobody saw. The room smelt like old shoes and stale sweat, but it was a familiar and comforting smell. Taking two deep breaths, she stood, ready to fake her way through her afternoon.

Heading for the door, she was barely paying attention as it swung open, almost hitting her. It was Carla, one of the sales managers. In fact, she had been Chloe's manager before she was promoted to the design team. Although the two only had a work relationship, they were on friendly terms. Carla's dark, almond eyes had a mischievous glint in them, her dark, straight hair bouncing as she moved. She laughed as she swung open the door, "Oops!"

Carla met eyes with Chloe and her face immediately changed. Chloe's stomach sunk as she realised that she wasn't holding it together as well as she thought she was. Carla reached towards her, touching her hand, which Chloe pulled away, stepping backwards. She felt her emotions bubbling over uncontrollably. No, no, no, she pleaded with herself, turning in a vain attempt to hide it from Carla.

"Babe," Carla said softly. Chloe had always hated that Carla called her that, but today the familiarity of it was comforting. Chloe opened her mouth, trying her best to form the words "I'm fine," but only managed to make a mournful squeak. Her throat closed up as her eyes spilled over, the warm tears running freely down her face. Swallowing the lump, she managed to say "Sam."

Sam and Chloe were high school sweethearts. They had been together seven years, since they were seventeen. Their relationship was the longest of the friendship group, and the others had looked to Chloe for advice with their own relationships. Chloe had completed an interior design degree to compliment his in architecture. They had planned to create a firm together, as husband and wife. They had even talked about venues for their wedding, and names for their kids. Chloe had her whole life planned out with Sam. But all that had changed two days ago, on Saturday night.

Carla grabbed Chloe, pulling her into a firm hug. She didn't say anything, but her touch was all it took for Chloe to break under the weight of her pain. She was blubbering now, opening weeping against Carla's shoulder.

Leaning her face on her hand, Chloe shook her head to bring herself back to the present. As she pushed the uncomfortable memory away, the day she broke down in Carla's arms, she glanced over at her notebook, which was open to her completed to-do list. Chloe had worked for this company for four years. It wasn't a difficult job, at least not for her. Work was a happy place now for the Chloe, compared to her two-bed villa. At twenty-five, Chloe had expected her life to be a little different. In fact, until ten months ago, everything had been going well. She leaned back in her chair and took a deep breath, staring up at the textured ceiling. She was not about to let herself be affected by that memory, not now. With only hours left of her work week, she realised she was looking at another weekend alone. No plans, a bottle of wine and a pile of laundry.

An enthusiastic tap on her shoulder bought her out of her reverie, and for a second, she thought she had been caught slacking off, and her chest tightened. Glancing up though, she saw the beaming smile of Carla. As she leant her slender frame against Chloe's desk, her tan arms folded in front of her chest, she smirked, brimming with the obvious urge to share gossip. Chloe had never been much for gossip, but right now, she was keen for any excuse to escape her thoughts. She lifted her bulky headphones, resting them around her neck.

"What do you want?" Chloe said with feigned annoyance, but failed to hold in a smile. Carla had to stifle a laugh.

"I was wondering if I could run some ideas for a new design past you," Carla said flatly. A lie. She lowered her voice as she leaned in, her straight black hair falling gently forward as her eyes lit up. "The new starters are getting the walk through now."

Carla somehow managed to balance the ridiculous pressures from head office, the needs of her staff, and still run the most profitable and friendliest department in the store, and somehow still found time for Chloe. On her first day, Carla proudly showed off a photo in her locker of her being held up by two shirtless firefighters. If there's one thing Carla loved, it was a hot, muscly man. One in uniform was even better. It wasn't the first time Chloe had been roped into escorting Carla on her on one of these eye candy scouting missions. In fact, it was becoming something of a ritual of late. Carla had initially given Chloe some space since she had become single, but had decided around the six-month mark that enough was enough, and that Chloe needed to get back into dating, despite her protests.

Chloe sighed, setting her headphones down on her desk. She wasn't sure she was in the right mood for another of Carla's boyfriend scouting missions. "Carla, I don't know..."

With a wave of her hand her friend cut her off. "Come on Chloe. It's just a bit of fun."

Chloe pressed her lips together. She knew there was no point in arguing, even if she felt uncomfortable. "I just..." she struggled to smile as she stood up from her desk. "Okay."

"Don't worry hun," Carla said, her face softening as she placed her hand on Chloe's. "I got you."

Tears welled up in Chloe's eyes. She couldn't help but be right back in that moment, ten months ago, storming out of Sam's house. It was if she was feeling it for the first time again, the painful swelling in her chest, the lump in her throat. The horrific crushing loneliness as she realised that she had nobody she trusted enough to call for support. Carla was standing now too, and took her hand with a sympathetic smile, bringing her back to reality. She realised she had moved her hand across her chest, and quickly dropped it.

"Carla I-" she struggled, swallowing hard to try steady her voice. "Whatever. I'm not about to let Julie see me like this." Blinking to hold the tears back, she followed Carla out of the room.

"Okay so I really think there's one in this group you'll like," Carla said, a bounce in her step, obviously forcing a change in tone. Once they were out of earshot from Chloe's manager, Julie, they could talk freely without worry of being reprimanded for skiving off work. Even though there was no work to do, Julie always made a point of stressing that everyone needed to look busy. It annoyed Chloe to no end the amount of time and effort wasted on appearances, but perhaps that was misplaced bitterness. Carla turned to Chloe and levelled her with a meaningful stare and a cheeky grin. "I saw them all in the lunch room when I went to get my coffee. Just your type. Tall and broad."

"Oh, stop." Chloe said, blushing a bit, a genuine smile forming on her face. Carla had gathered Chloe's "type" from lunch time conversations about celebrities. Sam was in no way tall and broad, but she couldn't imagine herself ever being with someone remotely like him again. The very thought of another rail thin man touching her made her stomach churn. Even still, she was still not used to the idea of finding someone else attractive, having been in a relationship where she felt extreme guilt for even thinking about someone other than her boyfriend. *Seven wasted years,* she thought sourly. Since the breakup, she had questioned everything she knew about herself. Chloe had put her trust in someone, and now, without him, she didn't really know who she was.

Every time there were new starters, there was always a handful of guys Carla found attractive, the fit and muscly type, preferably covered in tattoos. She would drag Chloe from her desk to look at them, and time and time again Chloe would play along, mostly to humour Carla. The truth was, Chloe didn't even really know what her type was. After all, she had been in a relationship since she was a teenager, and the world of adult dating was foreign to her. It was safer to go home alone, stick to her routine.

Carla was leading her down the hallway, where there was a large window from the second floor which overlooked the first. You could very easily spot someone from that point if you were looking for them. Chloe smiled softly as she watched her friend who, almost nose to glass, was eagerly scanning the floor for the group. Even with just the lightest touch of mascara, Carla was stunning. She had treated herself well, which was evident in the lack of lines on her face. Many people guessed her to be twenty-seven, when in fact she was closer to forty. -"I saw them heading towards the stairwell a few minutes ago. They can't have gone far yet."

Chloe gave one quick sweep of the lower level, but didn't see anything of note. This was more Carla's thing than hers, anyway. Not knowing what she was looking for except for a group of people, she glanced off to the side with a content sigh. *Are you up to uniform standard?* The new sign had finally been installed next to the mirror, another initiative from the big bosses. She caught her own reflection next to it. There was nothing really remarkable about Chloe, she was the average height, pale, with green eyes underlined with bags and freckles. A curvy figure, with a full chest, soft stomach and wide hips, the kind a magazine would call "hourglass", even though she was no painted pinup. Her whole life she had been a little bit bigger than was fashionable, but that hadn't really bothered her. She had always taken comfort in knowing at least one person wanted her. *Except he doesn't,* she thought, almost reflexively. The uniform fit her a bit awkwardly, as most women's clothing did, pulling tight across the chest and then looser around her middle, the pants fitting snugly around her hips but gaping at the back of the waist. To top it all off, the red of the shirt made her skin look sallow. Her dyed black fringe was a little too long and hitting her eyebrows, the rest of her hair piled on top of her head in a messy bun. Her eyebrows probably needed to be reshaped at this point. *My god, I look tired.* She hadn't slept very well for months.

With a breath she pushed the intrusive negativity from her mind, pulling at her shirt. Being alone in her bed at night was torture, the darkness and silence pressing in and making her feel horribly alone. So, she had found herself staying awake much too late with the TV on, trying to help her forget she was completely alone. Sometimes she even found herself falling asleep in the living room, waking up crumpled in the cushions. She ran her hand over her smooth cheeks. The tiredness wasn't only from her lack of sleep; feeling alone and miserable had worn her down. *Maybe I just need to invest in some bronzer.*

"There!" Carla squeaked, pointing a little too enthusiastically. Chloe followed her gaze and saw a group of about 15 people on the lower level, emerging from a warehousing aisle near the back of the floor. They were too far away to make out anyone clearly, but Chloe did spot a tall, broad figure in the crowd. *Maybe there's hope this time.*

Before she could get a better look at anyone, or even open her mouth to say something, Carla had grabbed her wrist and was speeding down the stairs. It was hard to believe this woman was more than ten years her senior, but Carla's carefree enthusiasm was rubbing off on Chloe, who found herself cracking a smile as she followed. They rounded the corner at the base of the stairs and saw the group across the floor. Their backs were to the women, but you could hear Dan, from Human Resources, explaining about the importance of safety to the crowd. With a booming authoritative voice, Dan was constantly stuck with giving the first tour to new staff, a task which he was often heard lamenting about. But with the other HR staff member being a rather quiet women, his voice was the only one that would carry over such a crowd, and the hustle and bustle of the store.

Without a word, Chloe pulled up her notebook and pen, and Carla began a well-practised routine, walking to a nearby display and feigning thought, dramatically placing her hand on her chin. She started a conversation about increasing sales from that area, and caught a sideways look from Dan. Carla smiled back cheekily, and Chloe thought she saw Dan roll his eyes. It was kind of amazing that he let her get away with stuff like this, but being as good as she was at her job came with some allowances. From the display, both women were almost at Dan's shoulder, allowing both of them to get a look at the faces of the group.

Immediately Chloe saw the man Carla meant. He was just over six foot tall, but not by much, with broad shoulders. He was standing with his arms crossed, wearing a clean, black polo shirt and faded blue jeans. As he was listening to Dan speak, his face rested in a bored grimace. A good head above the crowd of much shorter women, Chloe could clearly see his face; short brown hair and stubble. He looked a bit like a slob. She gave Carla a despondent look.

"It does have some potential though, don't you think? Maybe a few small changes could really make it look better." Carla glanced over at the guy, indicating to Chloe that she was really talking about him. Chloe folded her arms, shoulders tense. Just imagining having feelings for someone again made her chest tighten. It was easier to act not interested than admit that she was still mending her broken heart.

"I don't think so. Maybe we just need something else entirely."

Carla shrugged with an apologetic look, and with a last glance and cheeky wave to Dan, disappeared into the aisle, taking a shortcut back to her department. Chloe definitely caught a sigh of annoyance from Dan, who had finished talking and the group had started to move to their next stop in the opposite direction. Chloe closed her notebook and tucked the pen she had been pretending to use into her bun as she watched the group leave, the guy in question bringing up the rear of the group. *I'm just not ready,* Chloe thought, glancing at her watch with a sigh. *It was okay to not be ready to leap headfirst back into love,* she reasoned with herself. She noted that she had at least wasted a good half hour on the fruitless escapade. Only an hour and a half to go.

Chapter 2

Leaning back in her chair as she sipped her mimosa, Chloe stretched out like a cat in the warm sun. It felt so good to be able to treat herself to things she really enjoyed. And there was not much Chloe enjoyed more than mimosas and brunch on a Saturday morning. It was a warm morning, and she was wearing her favourite dark grey maxi dress, which hugged her body gently and was thick enough material that she did not have to wear a bra, which was a godsend. Flat sandals and a sheer black kimono completed her look. She was wearing a small amount of makeup today with hair down, freshly washed after a night of beauty maintenance. She had got into the habit of putting effort in to her appearance on the weekend. Although told herself it was because she might meet someone, in reality her worst fear was to run into her ex, and have him see her looking less than her best. The amount of effort and stress that she put into attempting to look effortless and content was almost laughable. *It has only been ten months*, she reasoned with herself.

Relaxing back into her chair and placing the glass down on the table, she sat for a moment watching her friend Stephanie arrange the centrepiece, her plate of food, and coffee just so, and stand above it to snap the perfect photo on her phone. It made Chloe smile a bit to see someone have such an appreciation for food. Although many people thought it was self-centred or vain to share pictures of their food online, Chloe understood that how something is presented can make all the difference between it being wanted or not, and she appreciated that Stephanie understood that too, even if that was the only thing they really had in common.

Stephanie and Chloe were in the same friend group, but only because Chloe's ex-boyfriend, Sam, had been friends with

Stephanie's husband, David, since high school. During Chloe and Sam's relationship, Stephanie had met, dated, and recently married David. The four of them had spent a lot of time together, and the two had grown to become friends. She was a petite girl, with auburn hair she kept fashionably short in a bob, accentuating its natural curls. She had wide, grey eyes, which gave her an innocent, doe-like took. Today she was wearing a light floral sundress and cardigan, which was typical of her. Chloe would never admit it to anyone but herself, but Stephanie seemed to have her whole life going to plan, which was fine while Chloe's was too. But since the breakup, Chloe had found herself angry and jealous of Stephanie. She felt broken and lost since her relationship ended, but everyone in that friend group seemed to just expect her to continue on as normal.

Chloe was proud to say she's the kind of person who will try anything once, although that theory had never really been tested. She started dating when she started high school, and had very rarely said no to any teenage experience. She used to jump at the chance to play silly games like "spin the bottle" or "seven minutes in heaven". She had thought that sort of teenage sexual liberation was pretty normal until she met Stephanie, when they were eighteen, who was the polar opposite. It wasn't because of any religious upbringing, but Stephanie had always been more reserved in this way, opting out of the games and sitting quietly during drunken rounds of "never have I ever". On her hen's night, Stephanie had revealed that David was the only person she'd ever slept with. In fact, he was the only person she had ever kissed. For Chloe, the very idea of it sounded horrifying. Although her relationship with Sam had started in high school, she had had her teenage fun with enough people to know that he was pretty decent in the bedroom. *I would have been content with the idea of spending the rest of her life with him.* She thought, a slight sadness creeping over her.

With a swipe and a click her image of her warm pumpkin salad on dark stoneware plates was posted, Stephanie sat her phone down on the table beside her and filled her fork with leaves. Stephanie had quite a following on her Instagram as a food blogger, which is probably why she had chosen this new café for brunch. It was in the side of a laneway, with black painted brick walls, and rusted garden implements hung for decoration. The lighting was dim, coming only from decorative halogen globes strung artfully on long cables across the ceiling. To top it off, they had installed a garden wall running the length of the café. To Chloe's trained eye, it screamed pretentious and showy; not really her style. Chloe went straight for her poached eggs, slicing open the soft yolk and letting it seep through her sourdough bread. There was nothing better in this world than perfectly cooked eggs on fresh sourdough bread. This place might not have the design to be warm and inviting, but the food certainly made up for it.

"Have you been seeing anyone?" Stephanie asked, with an expectant face. "You know, since you guys split up?"

Chloe shook her head, mouth full of bread and egg. "I talked to a few people but, you know." Stephanie nodded, and took a bite of her salad. A silence hung in the air between the two women. The conversation so far this morning had been stunted and strained, and Chloe was getting a very weird vibe. She was trying her best to dismiss it, tell herself she was being overly sensitive. Stephanie had not really talked to her much in the past months since the breakup, and they had drifted apart. Chloe had come to terms with the fact that she had been rejected not only by Sam, but by his friends and their wives. She was the one on the out now. Initially it had made her mad, especially because it was no secret that the breakup was quite dramatic. In her mind, it would have been fairer for their friends to have taken her side. But mostly, they didn't. So, she had pushed them away, hurt, and become almost a recluse, declining events to parties that Sam was also invited to on principal. Even though she felt a bolt of power and confidence every time she declined, that feeling was short lived, and vastly diminished when she saw all the photos from her friend's fun night appearing on social media while she had been staging her solo protest at home, alone. Nobody ever seemed to miss her.

The feeling that something was amiss started to creep back, and she was starting to feel a bit apprehensive about this whole brunch situation. Telling herself she was being paranoid, she tried to focus on eating her eggs and not letting the mimosa go to her head. When she had received the text from Stephanie, she had assumed the whole group of girls would be coming. She was elated to be able to catch up with everyone, to be included again. But when she had turned up this morning, she was surprised it was only Stephanie and herself. *Maybe she was just waiting for the drama to die down to reconnect with me,* Chloe thought hopefully. She couldn't help but be a tiny bit hurt that someone she thought of as her friend hadn't been there for her when her world collapsed, but she had chalked it up to Stephanie not really being her friend to begin with. But now, Stephanie had asked her out and made an effort, so Chloe was determined to not be petty. Honestly, the invitation had made her feel wanted again, something she had been desperately missing. Sam had undermined her confidence throughout their relationship, taking her from the bubbly, independent teen to the woman she was today, tragically dependant on others for validation. Chloe had become acutely aware of it through many lonely nights of reflection, and she deeply hated herself for it. But she just didn't know how to escape the quagmire of self-doubt.

"Why not?" Stephanie probed, eyeing Chloe expectantly. Chloe was struck by the lack of warmth in the big grey eyes staring intently at her. Chewing on her salad, it was almost an accusatory look

Stephanie was giving her. It was making Chloe feel rather uncomfortable. "After all, it's been almost a year."

Chloe swallowed, taking a second to try put her words together. *I'm imagining it*, she told herself. *She's your friend. Stop being ridiculous.* She took a deep breath. "It's difficult after-" Chloe cut off, her throat involuntarily slamming shut around her words. Maybe it was the mimosa, but a wave of icy cold ran through her body, like someone had dumped cold water on her head. All of a sudden, she was back there, in that moment, when the truth came out. The icy feeling of absolute terror filled her, the same as when she had got that Facebook message all those months ago.

Chloe was home on Saturday night, which wasn't unusual. Sam didn't like her going out without him, and he was at a party with his university friends. Really, Chloe didn't mind, she was more of a homebody anyway, preferring a night in over a night out. Besides, most of Sam's university friends Chloe didn't know, despite dating him from high school and though university. She had been busy with her own degree, and her own friends, never mind her weekend job, and just hadn't had much time to socialise with a bunch of students from a different university. If she had gone, she would have been awkwardly hanging by his side the whole night, which was just annoying for Sam. She didn't want to ruin his fun. Sam hadn't really made much of an effort to bring her along either, which didn't bother her. Being together for seven years, you kind of developed an understanding like that.

She had just got home from the gym, and was planning to spend the night watching Buffy reruns. Hopping out of the shower and feeling refreshed, her mind was on whether to order in pizza or cook something for dinner. It was getting pretty late and she didn't feel much like cooking. She had slipped into her sweatpants and oversized shirt, and braided her long hair to protect it from damage while she slept. She had to push her side swept fringe out of the way to apply her moisturiser, which annoyed her. She hated having a fringe, always having to push it out of the way, out of her eyes, and get it trimmed regularly. But that was how Sam liked her to look, so she kept it like that. Love was about making sacrifices, right? Having a fringe wasn't that much of a sacrifice.

She heard her phone buzz, and grabbed it, thinking it must be Sam wishing her a good night. To her surprise, it was a message from Jason, a high school friend she hadn't spoken to in over five years. Jason and Chloe had been almost best friends through high school, since they sort-of dated at age 13. It was a three month "relationship" which only amounted to a bit of innocent hand holding. They did grow close though, and were there for each other through the highs and lows of high school. But shortly after graduation, Jason had moved over east to pursue his career as a musician, and their contact had grown less familiar and less frequent. Now, she wouldn't know the first thing about his current life. She knew he had flown back over to visit, but usually he was too busy with family and the guys to catch up with her. Why would he be messaging her out of the blue on a Saturday?

I don't really know how to say this.

I'm sorry

There was a long moment where the three dots blinked on Jason's end of the conversation. There was no hello, nothing casual about this. Chloe's heart was pounding in her chest, stomach churning. Something was very wrong.

He's cheating on you, has been for 10 months.

All the guys know and just nobody wanted to be the one to tell you.

The pit of her stomach collapsed, her phone fell to the floor. Chloe had forgotten how to breathe. The world was spinning. She felt sick. Seven years. She didn't make a sound though, didn't cry, she was in too much shock. Only last week she and Sam had been looking at apartments to buy together. Her mind was whirling. Seven years and after all she'd done for him, all she had given to him. She had shaped her life around being a good partner for him. It was a lie. Chloe's emotions swelled from shock to anger. How dare he do this to her, to them? And it took Jason to tell her. All of them knew, for ten months, and they had just let her be led on, be fooled, be treated that way? She picked up her phone with shaking hands, ignoring the newly cracked screen, and called Sam, no answer. Of course.

Tears were brimming in her eyes as she scrolled through her contacts list, trying to find someone to call, to comfort her. Her entire life had been flipped on its head and she desperately needed a friend. Jason said they all knew, so who could she trust?

Chloe swallowed the lump that had formed in her throat, and suddenly all she could look at where her eggs. She wasn't crying, but every fibre of her being was enveloped in a deep sadness. Reliving that night, the whole ordeal, in a matter of seconds had knocked her a bit. And she had been reminded that on that night, one of the people she felt she couldn't call was Stephanie. Her life had just been ripped apart like an old bedsheet, she wasn't ready to clean up the edges. Not just yet. "It's a bit hard after what happened."

Stephanie seemed completely oblivious to the emotional rollercoaster Chloe had just experienced right in front of her, her doe eyes blinking blankly as she silently shifted her food around her plate and worked it onto her fork. I guess, not having experienced something like that herself meant she didn't understand the gravity of what went on. That night had been the worst night of Chloe's life, and finding out Sam had been cheating on her was just the beginning of it. She had told her friends he had cheated on her, but hadn't ever spoken about what happened after. Chloe felt a rush of anger, and tears welled in her eyes. She wanted desperately to tell Stephanie, in fact, to tell anyone who would listen, shout it from the rooftops, but had no idea how to put it into words. Somehow, she also felt that putting it into words would make it more real, and if she kept quiet, and never told anyone, she could forget it ever happened. With a mouthful of salad, Stephanie shrugged nonchalantly, and leaned back in her chair. With a pang of annoyance at how flippant Stephanie was being, Chloe tensed up, her emotions quickly receding and her defensive wall going up. She opened her mouth to say something, but hesitated, and instead stuffed the last part of her eggs in her mouth, but they had gone cold and now, and were nowhere near as enjoyable as they had been.

"Well," Stephanie perked up. "Did you hear what happened at Kyle's birthday?"

Another party Chloe was invited to, but declined. She still couldn't even think about the last time she saw Sam without being hit with a wave of emotions. She wasn't sure she could remain so composed, or hold her tongue if she saw him in person, especially if there was alcohol. Chloe wasn't a big drinker, but a few glasses of wine seemed to strip away the new foundation of emotional control she had built since the breakup. The very thought of it made her mouth dry, and all she could muster was a short "No."

Stephanie's eyes sparkled. Any hope Chloe had held for Stephanie becoming a closer friend to her was fading fast. It was becoming apparent that all she had asked her out for was to gossip, and probably because she was the only person who wasn't at the party, and didn't already know. Or because she expected Chloe to have a dramatic reaction, something she could talk about with the other girls. Stephanie seemed to revel in the drama of the small friendship group. At this moment the waitress came by to collect their plates, and Chloe ordered a second mimosa. She had a feeling she was going to need it. Stephanie asked for the waitress to prepare the second half of her salad to take home, and the plates were swiftly taken away.

Stephanie leaned forward on the table, one hand gently stroking her coffee cup, her face twisting into an excited smirk. This was the moment she had been waiting for, and Chloe could not be less enthusiastic.

"So, Sam was lying on the couch, totally drunk," Stephanie started, bubbling with excitement. Her eyes were sparkling, and the words fell from her mouth as if she just couldn't contain them anymore. Chloe's stomach formed a knot, she felt her jaw tense. She wanted desperately to leave, to get away from this conversation. She felt incredibly uncomfortable, but trapped. "And then Michelle, you know, Kyle's girlfriend, came in and lay next to him. Everyone went out to eat dinner and then David walked in half an hour later, and they were fucking!"

Chloe's jaw just about hit the floor. She never much liked Michelle, and in fact most of the girls from school had made up a cruel nickname for her. It suddenly occurred to Chloe that Stephanie had not been around then. Michelle had only been with Kyle a few months, but to cheat on him at his birthday party? That was a new kind of low. Chloe's voice was flat when she finally spoke, "Michelle cheated on Kyle at Kyle's birthday… with Sam?"
The sparkle fell from Stephanie's eyes, and her smile faltered. That

was obviously not the response she was seeking, or expecting. "Well, when you put it like that," Stephanie glowered, rolling her eyes. "That makes it sound kind of shitty."

That's because it is. Chloe stayed silent. *In what universe would she think I would be happy about this*? Chloe had also been the victim of cheating only months ago. How could anyone be so clueless and insensitive, let alone someone who is supposed to be a friend? Chloe's stomach churned and she put her second mimosa to her mouth, practically inhaling half the glass, and avoiding Stephanie's gaze. She was sure her rage was painted across her face, although she was trying her best to contain it. She wondered how many people Stephanie had gossiped and laughed over brunch with about her situation. How many times did her grey eyes light up about her misfortune? How many of them laughed with her? It made her feel sick.

Chloe looked back at her companion, who was leaning back in her chair, arms folded, almost pouting. This woman wasn't her friend, that was abundantly clear, and she was not making any effort at all to change that. Drama, and other people's pain, was nothing but entertainment for her. *Maybe she didn't know Sam had cheated?* Chloe thought, desperate to understand how someone she once considered a friend could be so insensitive. She had never actually told her herself, and who knows what Sam had been saying these past few months. He had proven to be an expert at deceit and manipulation. But the anger rising up in Chloe diminished any reasoning she could come up with for Stephanie's callousness. They really had absolutely nothing in common, and absolutely nothing to talk about. In that moment, all fondness she felt for Stephanie fell away. Chloe would probably never see her again after today, she was certainly not going to make any effort to on her side. Her rage settling into a heavy knot in her stomach, she readied herself for a confrontation.

The salad arrived back at the table in a neat little plastic container, looking dramatically less appetising than it had on the trendy stoneware plate, and Stephanie abruptly stood up to leave, her face expressionless. *Definitely not making any effort.* Chloe observed. With a sinking feeling, she realised that she had been hoping for Stephanie to reach out to her, to be a friend, to cement Chloe's own idea that she was wanted and lovable. She was disgusted with herself. Sam had really broken her, and Stephanie was just an extension of that cruel rejection. Levelling a steely gaze at the other woman, Chloe breathed through the last thin veil of fear that had been holding her back. Before she could stop it, the words tumbled out. "Stephanie, did you know Sam was cheating on me?" Stephanie slipped the salad in her bag, calmly looking at the ground. She showed no sign of surprise, it was almost as if she had been expecting the question. Chloe felt her face flush, but she held her tongue, waiting. It was obvious that she knew. It was a moment before she looked back at Chloe, and her grey eyes were cold. She seemed to be studying her, trying to read her. "Yeah. Sam told us all about it." Her voice was level, and flat. Chloe felt like she was being judged. *What the hell did he tell them?* Stephanie then tilted her head with a slight sarcastic grin. "Chloe, hun," she was condescending now, and Chloe felt a wave of rage. "You need to get over it. It's old news."

And then she turned, and left, before Chloe could respond. Tears welled up in Chloe's eyes, her body's only available response to yet another rejection. Staring down at the table, she watched her tears fall onto the black painted wood, rage and sadness swirling inside of her. She felt so small, pathetic and unwanted. Her chest ached. With a few deep breaths, she pulled herself up, wiped her eyes and the table calmly, and left the café.

Chapter 3

Chloe was at work early, as usual. She dropped her bag in the office, looked over her immaculately clean desk once, and walked down the hallway and into the small lunch room. The brunch with her former friend had shaken her, as well as given her a lot to ruminate about. Chloe was telling herself she had every right to be upset with how harsh and uncaring Stephanie had been, but at the same time was struggling to make sense of it. All she could think of was that she had never experienced anything like this, and so simply couldn't relate. Chloe shuddered as she remembered that only her therapist knew the whole story. In her therapy sessions, she had realised just how often Sam was on her mind. No wonder she hadn't been able to move even a single step forward into the rest of her life. Being aware of it now meant Chloe had more control over her thoughts, and had noticed an immediate difference in her mood, even if she did think about it pretty often still. It surprised her, how much more aware she was of the world around her now her head was not permanently in a Sam cloud. She was happy and bubbly again, for the first time in a long time, and it felt great.

She shook those thoughts from her head with a heavy sigh, and left the office to get a coffee from the pod machine. Work was no place to be getting emotional. Getting in early meant that not only could she take her time to organise herself for the day, and get her head straight, but she was sure to have peace and quiet pre-caffeine, which she needed today of all days.

The pods whirred, and Chloe ran her fingers through her hair to brush it, pulling it up on top of her head with a twisting action which made her bun relaxed, but controlled. She had been to her therapist and reflected on what Stephanie had said; *Get over it. It's old news.* It was incredibly harsh, but her therapist had managed to frame it in a different light. Maybe Chloe was spending too much time focusing on her hurt, on what happened to her, and it was trapping her in a routine of self-deprecation and self-pity. Sure, her world had been flipped upside down, but she had been spending the last ten months trying to figure out how to put it the right way up again, trying to get back what was. Perhaps instead, she needs to work with it how it is. Spending months grieving the life she had, and had planned on having with Sam was not doing her any good. She needed a new perspective. That insight had opened up a world of thinking for Chloe, which was both terrifying and exciting. The soil had been overturned, and she needed to plant her seeds to grow from this experience. The thought of the unknown was frightening, and she felt incredibly vulnerable allowing herself to drop her guard and let herself move forward. Taking a deep breath, she practised a mindfulness technique her therapist had taught her. She was here, now, in the present. Not in the past.

The liked the routine of mornings, it was calming and predictable. It set her up to have a good, productive day at work. She could smell the floral and fruity fragrance of her conditioner as she swept her hair up, and the tart bitterness of the coffee as it poured into her cup. Everything was calm. She was determined to not let another day go by in stuck her own mind. From today onwards she was going to open her eyes and look forward. With a determined nod to herself, she reached for the coffee another smell hit her nostrils, something she's never smelt before. Immediately her senses were heightened with this new addition to the usual routine. It was a warm, dark scent, which reminded her of wood and leather. An image sprang to her mind of a wealthy man's study, the kind you see in soap operas. Her stomach flipped, and she felt a tingle between her legs. That was a feeling she hadn't felt in a long time, and took her by surprise.

"Excuse me." He slid past her to get to the pod machine, his broad frame coming a little too close for strangers. His arm brushed past her shoulder as he placed his cup down, and it sent a ripple of warmth through her chest

A pang of guilt hit her, but she quickly pushed it aside. Taking a breath, she calmed herself. *It's been a long* time, she reasoned. *I'm a grown woman. There's nothing wrong with feeling this way.*

He lifted his head, and turned to smile at her as his coffee brewed. "What flavour did you get?"

Oh my god. Chloe's brain had somehow turned to mush, and forgotten the English language. This man looked completely different from the first time she had seen him, when Carla had pointed him out in the orientation group only last week. His scruffy hair had obviously been cut, now short on the sides and slicked back away from his face, with a fresh, sharp fade. His messy beard was not short and even, and seemed to be sporting an oil. It accentuated his soft jawline, giving it a manlier, mature look. She hadn't noticed before, but his skin was smooth, only sporting one mark she assumed was a mole near his right eye. His nose was only slightly bent, in a way that perhaps it was broken as a child. The uniform fit him well, Chloe thought, accentuating the broadness of his chest and shoulders, while also touching on the softness of his stomach. He was taller than her, but not so much that she had to strain to look at him.. "Uh, Vanilla."

He hadn't noticed her awkwardness, or if he had, he wasn't letting on. "I much prefer the Ristretto." His voice was a soft baritone, kind of smooth and round, of course he drinks a rich and bold Ristretto. Deep but gentle, he had the kind you would want to have read you an audiobook. Chloe's whole body was tingling as she stood there, unable to speak. Luckily, he broke the silence, "I'm Ezra. Ezra Stewart."

Chloe heard the rush of her blood pumping in her ears. She had never in her life felt like this before looking at a man, a pure physical attraction. "Chloe," she managed with a smile. She knew she had a beautiful one, having to suffer through braces to get it. She was silently thanking herself for taking the extra time this morning to put on some mascara and that bronzer. She gripped onto the warm coffee for dear life.

Ezra picked up his coffee casually and leaned against the wall. She noticed the muscles in the back of his hand move as he lifted his coffee to blow on it before sipping. The way his lips pursed was almost sensual.

Calm down Chloe, he's your co-worker. "You're new, right?" Chloe asked, blinking to try compose herself. "What department are you in?"

"Logistics, I'm in charge of refining the ordering and allocation process. You know, efficiency, basically." He smirked. "Heard your last guy didn't do such a great job of it."

"That's an understatement." Chloe sipped her coffee and raised her eyebrows, trying to seem nonchalant, even though she was acutely aware of her heart pounding loudly in her ears. Ezra had only been there a day and he already knew that office gossip. As the rumour goes, the last guy was eventually asked to leave the company after it became public knowledge that two different staff members were carrying his children. He had tried to woo Chloe as well, visiting her desk frequently to lay on the charm, but she had not been interested at all, and had found him quite sleezy.

"So," Ezra cocked his head, his blue eyes looking Chloe up and down. She almost felt the sensation run along her skin. His eyes lingered on her hips and chest just long enough for Chloe to notice. "You're in Design then?"

Chloe blinked. "Yeah, how did you know?"

"Everyone in Design wears their hair the same," he smirked, taking another sip of coffee without breaking eye contact. He wasn't wrong, almost everyone in Design was a woman, and had long hair kept out of the way in a messy bun. He leaned towards her slightly and added cheekily, "Plus, it says it on your badge."

Chloe felt her face flush, and instinctively looked down to her name badge pinned on her chest: Chloe Matthews, Design Specialist. *Of course.* Ezra laughed. "Well, I better get to it," he straightened up, and looked down the hall towards the offices, and Chloe thought she caught a hint of regret in his voice, almost as if he didn't want to leave. Maybe that was just her imagination though. "Guess I'll be seeing you around."

"Yeah, see you." Chloe nodded, words tumbling out of her mouth. Watching him walk towards the hall she became aware of his steady, purposeful gait. He was so aware of the space he took up, and he was confident. That must be why she felt this way. Chloe realised that she was grinning from ear to ear. *Maybe it's too early for me to fall back into love,* she reasoned, with a shiver of glee, *there's no reason why I can't enjoy looking.*

Chapter 4

The fluorescent lights buzzed and the air was getting stuffy in the small meeting room. Crammed in with the rest of the Design team, and the big bosses from the Sales department, Chloe was beginning to feel claustrophobic. Her chair was slightly broken, and the back was loose, so it would wobble wildly if she tried to relax into it. Why they didn't just replace it was a mystery to her, but she supposed they were just trying to keep costs down to make the annual profit as large as they could.- She hated these Thursday morning meetings, full of sales numbers which, according to the big bosses who hadn't set foot on the actual sales floor in months, told them exactly how they had to change their displays. Sometimes she just hated those big bosses. Apparently, they knew better than the Design team. Through her years of working there, Chloe had learned it was best to just do as you were told, and if it failed, so be it. If you tried to fight it, not only would you still end up having to make the changes, but the bosses would start to see you as a trouble maker. And that was never good.

Chloe stayed silent, sitting with her arms folded across her chest, and glanced around the room as the Store Manager, John, opened the floor to questions. If anyone had any, they were also staying silent, probably wanting to escape the room as much as she did. Finally standing up from the long table, Chloe only one item to change, which was a godsend. *Or possibly,* she thought bitterly, *I just know how to do my job.* As the crowd shuffled through the door, Chloe stretched her arms upwards, relieving the tension in her back. Dropping her arms, she glanced at her watch. She could go to lunch early, and make the changes later. Or she could quickly run down now, maybe end up being a bit late for lunch, but having the afternoon free to work on her designs. She only really needed to rotate one of the display cubes, which was heavy, but not exactly time consuming. With a quick glance down the hall towards the lunch room, where most of her colleagues were headed, she peeled off in the other direction to head downstairs to the floor. It would only take her a minute, and besides, she would prefer to skip the long line for the microwave that chewed into her break time.

She had been trying to bump into Ezra the entire week, but to no avail. She had just about tripled her coffee consumption, but each time he was either not there, or already chatting with other members of the Logistics team. Once, he had walked past her in the hall, smiled and said "Hey, Clo-", but he was well past her but the time she had processed a reply, obviously on the way to something important. It was almost like a fun little game to her, something small that bought her tiny pieces of joy throughout the day. It was completely innocent, of course, but the tiny bursts of adrenaline she felt when she saw him were lifting her overall mood. She had spotted the back of his head as he walked into meeting rooms, and even that had made her stomach do a backflip, but the more she turned thoughts over in her head of them together, the less overwhelming it became. Her overall better mood had somehow managed to trigger her long dormant lust, and her evenings had become less boring and depressing as a result. Although she would never tell a soul of how she had let herself fantasise about him. She was planning to pose the idea of them spending some time together outside of work, to get to know each other better. As friends, of course, they had only had one conversation over coffee. She didn't know the first thing about the guy, except for the way he made her feel.

Carla was midway through a sip of water when Chloe entered the department, her eyes widening as she saw her. Hurrying to put her water down on the tiny staff workstation, she almost spilt it, but caught it with a laugh. The staff workstation was really just a cupboard which housed their water bottles, some cleaning supplies, and a small desk for their notepad and a phone.

"Oh my god," Carla chuckled, placing her head on her arms in embarrassment. She collected herself with a breath, straightened up, and put her water bottle away. "Let me guess, you've just got out of the meeting and you need to change the new display."

Chloe shrugged, "Well, they forecast for the green boxes to sell as well as the white. And they haven't been, so now we have a backlog." Chloe rolled her eyes as she dropped her notepad on the desk. "It's not that big of a deal, John just wants me to rotate the display cube to face the aisle. It's a two second job."

"Didn't we tell them white always sells better than any colour in this market?" Carla groaned, and Chloe nodded. It's exactly what Chloe and Carla had predicted would happen, but again they weren't listened to. Again, they were the ones trying to contain the fallout. It was the same story over and over. Just then, the phone on the desk rang, and Chloe left Carla to answer. The display in question rose before her, a floor to ceiling mountain of white and green storage boxes, held together by fishing line and glue. Chloe spied the part she needed to move, a large cube which contained packaged stock for the customers to buy. Of course it was messily stocked, not at all appealing. She sighed, took a moment to ensure the path was clear, and gave the cube a solid shove.

It moved across the floor easily, but it was much heavier than Chloe had remembered. She walked around it, and she could already feel her blood pumping to her muscles, just like that had a hundred times before flipping tyres at boot camp. A second shove, and it was spun to face the right direction. Now, just one more to slide it back in to place, and she could go and get some lunch. If she was lucky, Ezra might be taking a late lunch today, and she might get the opportunity to speak to him. Chloe pushed hard, but the cube didn't move. Standing up, she could see the small foot on the base of the cube had become stuck in a tear in the linoleum floor. Her mind began drifting to thoughts of Ezra's deep laugh and delicious cologne, as she grabbed the top corner of the cube with her left hand and pulled upwards. The cube didn't move, but Chloe did. There was a rush of heat as she felt her shoulder separate from her arm, sweat poured from every pore and her breath caught in the mouth.

Her brain enveloped in panic, she concentrated on remaining calm, and not shouting or falling. She must have let go of the cube, because her arm slipped back in place with a sickening clunk. A wave of pain washed over her, radiating outwards from the socket, but almost drowning her in its weight. Chloe's stomach churned, and she focused desperately on not being sick. With an involuntary whimper, she knelt to the floor, her right hand supporting her left arm. Carla must have heard, because she was suddenly right in front of her. Chloe's mind was scrambled, but she could understand Carla saying something about calling first aid. Her friend gently took Chloe, who was now clammy and pale, and helped her lean against the offending cube. Chloe was barely present, and all she could manage was to nod to show she understood.

It seemed like both the next moment and forever when she saw the two pairs of boots arrive in front of her, and Dan's face appeared in her eye line. She smiled with relief. Her nausea had subsided a bit, and she had stopped sweating, even though her body was still covered in a thin layer. She would hate to see how her face looked, covered in sweat, tears on her cheeks, and pale as a ghost. Her mouth was dry and she was still in considerable pain, but the shock of the unexpected injury was wearing off, and Chloe had regained the use of her words. Focusing on keeping her breathing even, she explained to Dan what happened, and exactly how it had felt. He was nodding intently. "Sounds like a dislocation to me," he placed his hands on her shoulder. "Feels like its back in though, but it's really warm. You might have torn something in there." A second pair of hand was on her shoulder, slightly bigger but gentler than Dan's. A familiar voice said softly, "I'm just going to put a sling on you, if that's okay."

He didn't wait for an answer, which was a good thing, because Chloe's throat had suddenly closed in shock. She looked over, and there was Ezra, expertly folding the sling to support her shoulder. His brow was furrowed in concentration, his eyes full of concern. Her pain seemed to subside slightly as she was filled with that familiar spike of adrenaline at the sight of him so close to her. As he placed the sling over her arm, he leant in close, and his oaky scent filled her nostrils. She could feel his breath on her neck, the weight of his closeness making her heart flutter. Feeling a strange and calming sense of safety, the panic was fading and her heart rate slowing. Ezra finished tying the sling, gently rested his hand on her back. He said something to her, but she was starting to feel like she was falling, the world closing in around her.

The next thing she knew, Chloe was opening her eyes in a brightly lit room, flat on her back. Blinking a few times, she realised Ezra was sitting on a chair next to her, and she was flooded with embarrassment. She must have fainted, but she was disoriented, and couldn't quite remember why. She shifted to sit up, and realised her left arm was still in a sling. The incidents of the morning flooded back to her as looked around the small white room. It was only just big enough for the single bed across one wall, and a chair on the other, next to a small work station presumably filled with first aid supplies and forms. The entire room was filled with the smell of cleaning alcohol and Ezra's cologne. Pushing herself into a seating position, her body reminded her of why she was here. Her shoulder was still radiating pain, but that was secondary right now. Half-thoughts were forming in her mind, but she couldn't quite get anything intelligible to come out of her mouth. She was distracted, thinking about Ezra, and did something stupid. "Did I pass out or something?" She finally managed. Ezra's head snapped up from where he was looking, either at a form on the clipboard or at his phone, Chloe wasn't sure. An expression of deep concern was painted across his face. He shifted forward, casting everything in his hands aside, and steading Chloe with a serious gaze. "Yeah, you passed out." He said. "Did you eat today?"

"No," she replied, guiltily. She'd just had a coffee that morning, but was going to head to lunch right after she had fixed the display. She was slightly dizzy still, but her heart was pumping embarrassingly fast being this close to Ezra. And alone. Her face flushed with embarrassment, as if somehow he was going to find out all the silly, lustful things she had been thinking about him to herself.

Ezra leaned back in his chair and picked the clipboard up again. "I need you to fill this out, but considering you only have one working arm, I can write the answers in if it's easier?"

They went through the form, Chloe starting to feel less disoriented, and began feeling more comfortable in the small room. With each passing minute she was more confident that she was keeping her feelings under wraps. With Ezra there, and his deep, commanding voice, she felt safe. He even held the clipboard so she could sign it, having to move over to the bed next to her to do so. Despite the throbbing pain in her shoulder, her stomach was full of butterflies as she felt his warmth next to her. The smell of his cologne filled her nostrils, and her heart started beating faster. *He has no way of knowing you fantasise about him,* Chloe reminded herself. She steadied her breath and, in a moment of daring, tilted her head up to look at his face. To her shock and surprise, she met his gaze.

He quickly looked away, with an embarrassed chuckle. Heat flushed to Chloe's face as she realised he had been looking at her. A moment of silence hung between them as neither knew quite what to say. She watched him look absently at the clipboard in his hand, a look or determination brewing in his eyes. She had unconsciously moved her right arm to support her left in front of her chest, and was very aware of her breath. She was alone with Ezra. In a small locked room. Her heart jumped into her throat as she imagined him kissing her, his large hands caressing her body. *But that's never going to happen,* she reminded herself firmly, although now she was less certain of it. She was embarrassed, thinking like that with him right in front of her, as if maybe he could read her mind. But she was finding there was something about Ezra, something she couldn't quite put her finger on, that made her want to be less restrained, made her feel confident. He opened his mouth slightly to speak, but words seemed to catch and he shook his head, standing up with a sigh. "We should go and get some food into you. You'll feel better after you've eaten."

The room was so small, that Ezra was only about a foot away from Chloe, and now, with him standing up, and her sitting on the low bed, her face was level with his chest. She felt her gaze slide down his shirt, which sat snug over his soft stomach, over the thick, brown leather belt which hugged his hips, and to the subtle bulge in his uniform trousers. *Chloe!* She scolded herself, looking away and hoping he hadn't noticed her gaze. She had been allowing all sorts of thoughts into her head recently, allowing herself to feel the thrill of attraction. But that glance was enough to get her imagination racing. Her stomach tightened as she let herself wonder if he was entirely in proportion, being tall and broad. She felt a tingle of excitement between her legs, followed swiftly by a rush of embarrassment. This was not like her at all, to be thinking so sexually about someone right in front of them. It was only a fleeting thought, but it had ignited a primal desire in her, one which had been dormant a long time. She had unconsciously taken a step into unknown territory, and she was both terrified and excited. Taking a breath, she did her best to steady her thoughts and quell her emotions, not wanting her face to give her away.

She looked up to meet his gaze, and he offered her a hand to stand. She took it, which sent another wave of excitement through her body, and got to her feet. They were face to face now, so close that Chloe could smell the soft rose scent in his beard oil. Only inches apart in the tiny room, Chloe was finding it difficult to read his expression. He turned away, and reached for the doorknob, and the realisation that this moment was about to be over hit Chloe. She was expecting relief, but instead she felt a sudden wave of panic, the words just fell from her mouth. "Do you want to catch up for a drink sometime?"

He paused, hand hovering above the doorknob. She felt herself run hot with embarrassment. It was a moment before he turned back to her, a moment where Chloe was frozen, wishing the floor would just open up and swallow her whole. "Yeah, I'd love that." He said.

She had to be dreaming. There was no need for Chloe to pinch herself, however, as the ache in her shoulder reminded her, this was definitely real. Ezra turned to face her fully, interrupting her confused reverie. "I was going to ask you just before but I didn't want to come off, you know." He gestured to the room. Chloe nodded. It was a small room, he was a big guy, and she could see how that could be quite intimidating. Her chest tightened as she took in a deep breath to quell her emotions, and she caught his eyes flicker over hew figure, his soft, plump lips twitching into a slight smile. She could barely maintain the façade of normalcy.

Ezra seemed to suddenly come to, realising where they were, and nodded, turning his back to her while clearing his throat. "We need to get you something to eat. You're injured." He glanced over with a glint in his eye, and said before opening the door and stepping out. "We can talk about catching up this weekend over a sandwich."

Chapter 5

Chloe ran her hands through her hair she inspected her reflection in the rear-view mirror. Her hair was out, but she had moved the part from the centre to the side, away from how she had worn it habitually for years.

It was Saturday night, and she was on a date with someone her friends didn't know, and so her every move wouldn't be the subject of gossip over the next weekend. It felt incredibly liberating to have no expectations to live up to, nobody to compare herself to— nobody watching. Never mind the fact that this was the only real first date she had ever been on. She had started dating Sam in high school, after all.

And now, all of a sudden, she was sitting in her car outside the King's hotel, about to go on a date with the new guy. Chloe had chosen a simple black scoop neck shirt, which showed off her cleavage, and dark blue jeans for the occasion. She knew she had a great chest; she had caught many people looking at it, and it was one of her favourite pieces of her body. Besides, it made her feel beautiful and confident, which she needed today. Her stomach was tight with nervous energy. With one last fluff of her hair and a determined sigh, Chloe left the safety of her driver's seat and headed in to the unknown.

She saw Ezra before he saw her, sitting at a small table in the outdoor area, absently scrolling his phone, leg bouncing under the table, a pint of cider next to him. Deciding she also needed a drink, she stopped at the bar to order a gin and tonic. The bar was short, so she rose up on her tip toes as the bartender approached, and leaned forward to order. As she watched her drink get made, she focused on her breathing to calm her racing mind. *It's not that big of a deal, Chloe.* She repeated to herself. *It's just a drink.*

Closing her hand around the cool glass, she took one sip before stepping back from the bar. The tart bitterness of the tonic water met her tongue, accentuating the playful acidity of the lime. It might be considered an older woman's drink, but since trying one on a whim a few months ago, it had fast become Chloe's favourite. Savouring the flavour, she looked up to where Ezra had been sitting before, and her heart caught in her chest. He was looking directly at her. He smiled, and Chloe felt a rush, an echo of what she had felt in the first aid room days ago, but maintained her composure as she walked to the table.

Flustered, any witty first line she had prepared before evaporated from her mind as she reached the table, and the rich smell of that cologne met her nostrils. He placed his phone face down on the table as she approached, and clasped his hands together in front of him. He seemed to be holding his breath. She placed her glass down, and sat in the spare chair, managing to pull herself together enough to say simply, "Hey."

"Hey," His face brightened, and she could see relief flood his face too. The idea of his nervousness calmed her a bit. He raised his pint towards her. "Cheers to the weekend."

"Cheers," she replied, tapping glasses together. Taking a sip, she looked him up and down. He was wearing a plain, forest green t-shirt, which hung loosely about his body. The deep green tones made his eyes seem even bluer. He too had opted for jeans, well-fitting and clean. She rested her eyes on his face, and he was looking across the street as he drank from his pint. In the sunlight, she could see flecks of red hair through his beard. Somehow, he was much more attractive now, outside and out of the uniform. Chloe's heart was pounding in her ears, her stomach still fizzling nervously. Ezra glanced over at her, and smiled sweetly. *I can do this,* she reassured herself. She felt her entire body let go of the tension it was holding as Ezra started the conversation. "So, Chloe. Tell me about yourself."

"Well," Chloe started, laughing. "Where do I start?"

Ezra smiled. "How about we get the standard questions out of the way? Siblings, pets?"

"One brother, and no." She sipped her drink. "And this is the first real first date I've been on."

Ezra's eyes widened, "No! But you're gorgeous. I don't believe it."

"Ah, I just got out of a long-term relationship." She laughed, and shrugged. *Ah shit, I've bought it up already.* With a tinge of panic, she blurted out "and by recently, I mean ten months ago."

He nodded, leaning back in his chair. "I get that."

What the heck does that mean? She nodded, sipping at her drink. *Damnit Chloe, you've made it awkward.*

"What did he do to lose you?" Ezra said casually, sipping his drink. Chloe's face flushed, and her voice caught in her throat. She looked down at her hands, cupping her glass, and realised she was clenching her teeth. "I'd rather not talk about it."

There was silence. She chewed on her lip, chest tight. She hated how even the mention of Sam could still affect her so much. She just wanted to have a good time, a drink, with someone new. And here he was, still messing it all up for her. *That's it,* Chloe thought defeatedly. *I've gone and fucked this up already. I should have just stayed home.*

But, when she looked up at Ezra, he wasn't staring at her angrily, or bored. He was smiling softly, head slightly tilted, seemingly studying her face and chest. *Maybe I still have a chance*, she thought, relaxing a bit.

"Well, I've got a brother and no pets too," He laughed, breaking the silence. "So I guess we have that in common."

While Chloe's brain ran wild searching for something to say, she couldn't help but stare at his biceps, tight against his shirt sleeves. The delicious smell of his cologne was intoxicating, and incredibly distracting. *Say something,* she willed herself, but that only made her more anxious. As she scrambled for a topic, she was acutely aware of the silence going on uncomfortably long.

"Okay, how about a more serious question." His baritone voice was soothing as he leaned forward and looked into her eyes, making her heart skip anxiously. He didn't seem to mind the awkward silences. "Star Wars or Star Trek?"

She smiled, her body relaxing. He didn't take himself too seriously, and that put her at ease. Chloe was enjoying herself fully for the first time in a long time. "Star Trek, obviously."

He beamed. "I knew you were a good one."

He slid his hand across the table to touch hers. His hands felt strong, but he was purposely gentle as he traced his fingers affectionately down the back on her hand. She felt herself melt. She had imagined what his touch felt like countless times, but the reality was better than she could ever have imagined. She smiled, a tiny nervous laugh escaping her lips, as his fingers softly slid themselves between hers. They were thick, masculine fingers, slightly rough from physical work. He smiled, his voice dropping in to a more serious tone. "I've been wanting to do that for weeks."

Chloe was taken aback. *Was he really that in to me?* She thought, as she tried to come up with a response. All she could think about was how his hand would feel tracing up the soft skin of her thigh, how that rich baritone voice would sound in her ear, those soft lips kissing her neck. *What is wrong with you?* She scolded herself. Having locked away all her lustful thoughts for months seems to have made her hyper aware now she was letting herself feel them. She had thought she was fine alone, but with someone in front of her, obviously interested in her, she was beginning to realise that maybe she needed more. She nodded, and managed to stutter, "Uh, yeah, me too."

An hour passed, maybe two, the conversation flowing easily. She was sipping on a coke now, gently drawing circles in Ezra's palm. Any fear or nervousness she had heading into this date was long gone, replaced with a calm, warm attraction. Chloe was leaning on her left hand, hair falling around her face. Her eyes were spending more and more time watching Ezra's lips move, and wondering if they felt as soft as they looked. It had been so long since anyone had paid this much attention to her, let alone touched her so softly, and showed any real interest in her. The sun had gone down, and the bar had started to get busier.

The way he was looking at her made her skin tingle. Under the table, she felt one of his feet slip in between hers. She smiled at her, gauging her reaction, before moving his leg forward between hers. He rested the weight of it on her thigh, and Chloe felt a bolt of excitement shoot through her. The gentle pressure of his thigh against hers, even through both their jeans, sent her imagination wild. Images of him between her legs, her thighs wrapped around his naked waist flooded her mind. He was laughing as he lifted his glass to his mouth, and it was obvious he knew exactly what effect that had had on her. It was becoming more and more difficult to have a conversation.

"Do you think, maybe —" she started, and his eyes met hers. She felt the muscles in her stomach tense and she grasped at breath. "We should get out of here?"

His eyes lit up, and for a second, she thought she saw an expression of surprise on his face. Heart pounding in her chest, she was in uncharted territory. She saw no reason not to go someplace so she could kiss him, run her hands through his beard, and feel him holding her close. The thought of it, of her thoughts becoming a reality seemed too good to be true. There was a part of her that was waiting to be let down, but that part was steadily shrinking.

A smile brightened Ezra's face, as he stood from the table and took her hand. The crowd parted easily for his broad frame as he led her through. As they stepped out onto the footpath, Chloe realised just how cool the night had become. The crisp air kissed her skin, and she wasn't sure if the tingle she felt was from the cold, or nervous excitement. Ezra had walked to the bar, his place being only a few blocks away, so was shrugging into a heavy coat. She stepped towards her car, but Ezra hesitated for a second.

"Should we go back to mine," Chloe offered, smiling sweetly through her racing heart. "Maybe watch a movie?"

She caught the look on Ezra's face, and he seemed to be deep in contemplation. That wasn't at all the look Chloe was expecting, although what she was expecting exactly, she wasn't sure. Enthusiasm maybe? He nodded, almost sullenly and she unlocked the car, sliding into the driver's seat. She was trying not to read too much into it, but his expression made her confidence falter, and planted a seed of doubt in her mind. *It could be anything*, she told herself. Was she reading too much into it? Probably, she had been doing so much of that that recently. *You're just letting your insecurities get the better of you*, she told herself, but she only half believed it. As the car shuddered to life beneath her, she glanced over at the broad man in the passenger seat. He was smiling softly now, but quiet, and the rush of attraction she felt for Ezra returned.

"I need you to pull over."

The air felt warm inside the car, or maybe that was just her heart pounding in her chest. Chloe hadn't been looking at Ezra, keeping her eyes on the road, but about five minutes in he had placed his hand on her knee and broken the silence. She was shocked, and a bit confused, but they were just coming up to a suburban park, so she steered her hatchback into one of the parking bays.

Turning off the engine, her mind scrambled for what she had done wrong, so she could apologise for it. Had she been too caught up in her own fantasies to recognise some sort of sign? He was going to pat her thigh, tell her how she had messed up, get out and leave. She knew it all too well, Sam had done that more than once. *Of course,* she thought to herself with resignation, feeling his hand leave her leg. She was still looking directly ahead, shoulders tensing, readying herself. Suddenly, she felt his hand brush against her face, gently cupping her chin. Her eyes widened – this was not what she was expecting at all. She let him turn her face, his blue eyes meeting hers. In the dappled streetlights, they almost looked like tiny oceans. Then, before she had time to react, he was kissing her.

A dizzying excitement overwhelmed her, and she could feel the rough hairs of his beard scratching against her face, his soft lips on hers. It was awkward, being strapped to the seat, but she managed to unclip her seat belt and face him better, leaning in to the kiss. His lips were as soft as she had imagined. She breathed heavily as she ran her fingers through his beard, over his cheekbones, into his hair. He let out a soft grunt against her lips, which made her crotch tingle. The sound of him enjoying himself was like a switch in Chloe, she was getting lost in him.

Any thoughts of sensibility or restraint dissipated from her mind. She pulled back, her chest rising and falling heavily, to search his face. It was an Ezra she had not seen before. He looked hungry, and his eyes were aflame with a primal urge. His hand was on her chest, all gentleness gone. She let out an involuntary moan as his finger brushed her nipple, and she felt him perk up next to her. She could feel the heat of his breath on her neck, heavy with arousal. Pulling his face to hers she kissed him again, pushing her body against his as much as she could in the front of her small car. Her chest thrust forward as he slipped his hand into her shirt, unclasping her bra, the cool night air causing her nipples to immediately harden. He ran his warm hands over her soft skin, his eyes dropping to watch his caresses. Her chest was pale and supple in the streetlight. Her mind was swimming, eyes were drawn to his jeans, where an obvious bulge was now straining against the zipper. Her heart skipping, Chloe reached towards it, her fingers lightly tracing the length of his penis over his pants. She felt it twitch at her touch, which sent another ripple of excitement through her. Her body seemed to be completely in control now, as she felt herself panting with arousal. Ezra moaned eagerly, cupping her breasts in his hands, engrossed in her. She imagined his cock springing free from his jeans, allowing her to wrap her hand around its girth, and was suddenly overcome by an urge to taste it. Chloe carefully unbuttoned Ezra's jeans and slipped her hand into the waistband of his underwear.

As her fingers slipped under the elastic, Ezra suddenly launched himself back into his seat and Chloe pulled her hand back, startled. His eyes were cast down, and he lifted his hands to cover his face. Chloe was not sure what to do, sitting in her driver's seat with her breasts exposed, her eyes searched wildly to try and make sense of this reaction. Her lust began to quell, and thoughts trickled back in to her mind. Questions began bombarding her as she searched for what she had done wrong. She wanted to apologise, but didn't know what for. She clumsily started stuffing her breasts back into her shirt as her mind swam. In her desperation she couldn't find anything that made sense, but the longer they sat in a still silence, the more all-consuming her anxiety became. "Ezra, I'm sorry, I'm not sure what I did but –"

"No!" Ezra said, face still covered with his hands. Chloe went quiet, waiting nervously. "I have to tell you something. I wanted to wait for the right moment but it never happened and now," he swallowed, dropping his hands to his lap. He was avoiding looking at her. "I feel like I would be taking advantage by not telling you this."

Chloe levelled him with a stare, stomach sinking. She was not sure what was coming but she was pretty certain the tryst was over. Ezra was still visibly erect, and lost in thought, seeming to be trying to put the words together just right. Chloe took a deep breath to steady herself, pointedly looking away from his crotch. She realised she had tensed her shoulders, and was crossing her arms on her chest out of habit. Dropping her arms, she willed herself to relax.

"Chloe, I'm new to this, so I'm sorry I wasn't more upfront." Ezra locked eyes with her, placing one hand on her thigh. The same action he had done just moments before while they were driving, but this time she flinched. There was a different tenseness in his grip now. He swallowed nervously, but didn't speak again straight away, letting the tension hang in the air uncomfortably. Chloe held her breath as he spoke. "We decided to try something new, ethical non-monogamy."

We. He said we. Chloe's stomach dropped. "What do you mean, we?"

He sighed, leaning back in his seat and pulling his hand from her leg. He had heard the disappointment in her voice. "My girlfriend, Avery."

Chloe's mouth dropped open, but no words came. Her thoughts vanished as disappointment replaced them. In a matter of seconds, she had gone from aflame with passion to ice cold. All she could think of was Sam's ten-month affair, and how destroyed she had been when she had found out. A cold panic came over her, followed by a feeling of utter disgust. She couldn't do this. She couldn't be the other woman. Suddenly she wanted to be as far away from him as possible. To get out of the car and run into the night. She pulled back from him as much as physically possible while still in the driver's seat of her car. "No, no, I can't do this."

Ezra leant forward to grab her arm, to calm her. The ache from her injured shoulder stopped her from pulling away, and she looked up to his face. He was obviously confused by the extent of her reaction. "Chloe, I'm not cheating on her. She knows I'm on a date with you."

Chloe froze. *Ezra isn't Sam*, she reminded herself, and immediately felt the panic subside a little. Still, she narrowed her eyes at him. "Why should I believe you?"

Ezra sighed, but nodded. "I know, it's just my word, and considering the situation, it's easy to see how a guy could lie to get in your pants." He looked at her, his gaze steady, and she felt her icy barrier start to melt. Still, she kept a stony face. Still, she kept a stony face. "Would you feel better if you met her?" Chloe nodded before she had even had a chance to think. She still felt uneasy, and was going to need some time to process. This was not at all what she had expected. Tears were welling in her eyes, and, not wanting him to see, she turned back to start her car again. "Right now, I should take you home."

Chapter 6

Carla leaned forward and waved her hand in Chloe's face. "Earth to Chloe? You okay there?"

Chloe looked up from her lunch and blinked. She had been lost in her thoughts, again, about Ezra. Every lunch break for a week she had been sitting alone, turning the same thoughts over and over in her head and still not reaching a decision. *Ezra has a girlfriend, but they are open to seeing other people.* She just couldn't come to terms with how she felt about it.

She had done a complete flip on how she had been behaving before. Instead of chasing the thrill of seeing him in the hall, she had been actively avoiding Ezra for days. She just didn't know where they stood right now, and even though her heart still jumped into her throat when he passed her in the hall, and when she was wasting time on her computer, waiting for the clock to run down, she found her mind wandering back to last Saturday. The conversation had flowed so easily over drinks, they had got along so well. And then later, in the car, the way he kissed her, the way is touch made her feel, the sight of his erection through his jeans. Chloe had made a decision to be honest with herself, and if she stuck to that, she still wanted Ezra. She desperately wanted to hear him grunt and moan again, like he had in the car. The very thought made her shiver with excitement. It was a primal attraction, and her body ached for his. But her mind was a different story, and reality dictated that she couldn't just give in to her body. She was too unsure about his intentions. She barely knew the guy, and had no idea if he was being truthful. Was his girlfriend really okay with him seeing other women? Was she okay with getting involved in that? She honestly didn't know, and turning the question over and over in her head was only making her more confused.

"You've got something on your mind." Carla was eyeing her suspiciously as she sat down. "Spill, girl."

Chloe hesitated. She couldn't exactly tell Carla she was seeing Ezra. They worked together, and Ezra already had a girlfriend. Whether it was above board or not, the last thing she wanted was to become office gossip material. She had survived four years without any controversy. She took a mouthful of food to buy herself a few minutes. She really did need someone to talk to and help her sort out her feelings.

Chloe swallowed, and took a sip of her water, trying to be as casual as possible. "I matched with this guy on Tinder," she lied, avoiding eye contact with Carla. "We went out for drinks. Everything was going really well. We totally hit it off. But he told me he…" She paused, and looked directly at Carla, trying to read her reaction.

"What?" Carla said, narrowing her eyes. "He's got an STD? Kids?"

Chloe laughed, "No, no." She took a deep breath. This is it. Her body was practically vibrating with nervousness. "Have you heard about ethical non-monogamy?"

To her surprise, Carla nodded, leaning back in her chair and taking a sip of water. Her eyebrow was raised "So he's got a girlfriend?"

Chloe was shocked at how cool Carla was being. Was she just so out of the loop with adult dating that she was over thinking this entirely? Chloe was expecting some sort of surprise, a gasp maybe. But no, Carla, as usual, was calm. Chloe managed a nod, and took another bite of her sandwich, as she heard Carla tapping her finger on the table repeatedly as she pieced it all together. "And your last boyfriend cheated on you and you had no idea, so you don't want to go through that again."

Carla had been there for her the day after Chloe had found out about Sam, when nobody had answered their phone, or replied to her messages. She had felt so alone, until Carla swung that door open in the locker room. Since then, she had fast become Chloe's rock. Carla was the only person in the world, apart from Sam, and her therapist, who knew everything that had happened that night.

Chloe was standing in the parking lot, absolutely livid. She had arrived to the meeting spot early; she couldn't stand waiting around in this state. To pass time she had bought a coffee, but it was cheap, and the beans were burnt, so she was not drinking it. It tasted disgusting, like hot dishwater. Besides, her stomach was in knots.

Sam pulled up in his red Jeep wrangler, and immediately Chloe's eyes were daggers. She had found out only last week he had been cheating on her, and this was the second time since that she had seen him in person.

Maybe she was stupid for coming after what happened last time. She knew what this was about though, of course. He was going to apologise and ask her to come back. He's realised how important she is in his life. After seven years, and all the times she bent over backwards to help and accommodate him, how could he not? Cutting contact made him realise just how much he needed her. But she was ready to tell him to go shove it, she was better off on her own. She was putting on a brave face, but in reality, she was barely holding it together. This relationship was the only one she had ever known. She had shaped her life around Sam's career choices, picking a complimentary degree like her parents had suggested. It was supposed to be forever.Sam crossed the road towards her, looking downwards and avoiding eye contact. He was a thin man now, with a patchy beard and ratty, receding dark brown hair which curled on top of his head. He hadn't always been this way. A year ago, before he started going to these parties, he had been slender, yes, but fit, and his olive skin was always sporting a slight tan. His eyes used to sparkle like someone who was full of optimism, and laughed a lot. But he had changed. He wasn't the person she had fallen in love with. As he reached her, she noticed the smell of stale beer and cigarettes on him, as if he had worn his shirt out and hadn't bothered to change. It almost made her gag. No, definitely not the boy he used to be. He gestured for her to follow him, and she did, part of her annoyed he hadn't bothered to speak to her.

They sat on a park bench, not looking at each other. They were far enough away from other groups of people that nobody could hear them talk, but there were other people around. Chloe was clutching her coffee, unable to turn and look at Sam. Only two weeks ago they were planning their future together, and now he made her skin crawl. She was watching a young blonde woman, who was playing with her toddler on the grass, and felt a sudden pang of sadness. That wasn't going to be her any time soon. She lifted her cup to her mouth and took a sip, despite it tasting like garbage. Still was preferable than breaking the silence. Finally, Sam spoke. "You know why I asked you to come here?"

Chloe shrugged, attempting to convey an air of superiority, even though she was on fire with anticipation and rage.

Sam looked at her, but Chloe continued to look ahead. Attempting to seem unbothered, it also helped her focus on keeping her emotions under control. She was tensing her jaw so much it was beginning to ache.

"I need to tell you why I did it." He started.

"No way." Chloe couldn't contain a laugh as she said those words. He was unbelievable. This was not what she was expecting. "I don't care."

"You're just so..." Sam started, completely ignoring what Chloe had just said. "You aren't spontaneous enough, you know. You refuse to experience what it's like to have your mind opened. I just can't be with someone who's not..." he made a hand gesture like he was kneading invisible bread while he searched for the right word. "You, know, the right vibe."

Chloe's mouth was practically on the floor. What? How was this my fault?

Sam shrugged, running one hand through his filthy hair. "If you made an effort to change, I don't know, I might consider taking you back."

"Are you fucking kidding me?" The words fell out of Chloe's mouth before she could even think. She was enraged. "You cheated on me. For ten months. YOU fucked up. You want to clear your conscious by making it MY fault? You're pathetic."

Chloe realised she was on her feet, even though she didn't remember standing up. Sam was looking downwards, shaking his head with a smirk. He wasn't listening. He'd already decided he was justified in what he had done. "The right vibe?" she was no longer being able to control the volume of her voice. "What the fuck does that even mean?"

She was so angry she was involuntarily laughing, and tears were forming in her eyes. She was kind of stuck, her brain not properly working. She had an impulse to hit him, smack him right in his pathetic face, to throw her shitty coffee all over him and his filthy shirt. She imagined how good it would feel after everything he had done to her, everything he had put her through. But despite her overwhelming rage, she would never, not even to a wormy shit like him. "Goodbye." She muttered, not able to summon any better parting words. She was losing the ability to hold back her emotions and desperate to leave. She started walking off.

"Look I'm sorry." He said, seemingly unaware of the sarcasm dripping off his words. "Can I at least get a hug?"
Chloe scoffed, looking back at him. She felt such disgust for him, seeing him sitting slouched on that park bench, arms outstretched, offering her a hug. She turned, and just kept walking.

She was so angry that her strides were more like a power walk. She was doing everything in her power to keep it together, to get back to her car as fast as she could without running, before she let her emotions out. As she hit the car park, the sight of his red Jeep made her irrationally mad, and she lobbed her almost full coffee at it. She missed completely, the lukewarm brown liquid spilling spectacularly next to his back tyre.

She gritted her teeth in anger as she powered to her car, unlocking it as she approached. She just about yanked the door off its hinge as she got in, and slammed it shut. Then, finally alone, she started laughing again.

Tears were streaming down her face, and she was intermittently cackling with the absurdity of it all and pounding her steering wheel with rage. Seven years, so much time, effort, love and support, to be told it was her fault because she wasn't good enough? It was becoming painfully clear that he didn't care about her at all, and maybe never did. She was overcome with a drowning sadness, and just let herself weep freely, her face in her hands, animalistic wails escaping her mouth. It felt like someone had reached into her chest and torn her heart out. She wasn't sure how long she was there for, but after some time she was exhausted, and the overwhelming emotions finally subsided. She was able to wipe her face, her eyes red and puffy, and start her car to drive home. As she drove out of the car park, she noticed with a deep sense of finality that the Jeep was gone.

"I just don't know if I can do it," Chloe said, blinking tears from her eyes. The memories of the breakup were still haunting her, even when she was trying to move on.

Carla tiled her head, "You don't know if you want to do it, or if you should?"

Chloe tiled her head questioningly. "What do you mean?"

Carla leaned forward, levelling her with a serious gaze, her brown eyes caring. "What we want and what we *should* do doesn't always line up, right? But who made these rules about what is right and wrong, about how we *should* be living?" she paused for emphasis. "If you aren't hurting anyone, and you are happy, why shouldn't you do what you want? Being alone and miserable, you might take some comfort in being right. But you have the opportunity to be happy, maybe not forever, maybe even just for a little. And you want to run scared because of *should*." Chloe was nodding slowly. She'd never really thought about it that way, but it made a lot of sense. Carla broke into a smile "So the only question is: do you want to see him again?"

"I mean I want to; I definitely want to." Did she sound too enthusiastic? She hoped Carla hadn't picked up on that. "But I guess I'm just not sure I can trust what he says. I mean, he says his girlfriend knows, but how do I know it's the truth?"

Only days before she had found out about the cheating, Chloe remembers Sam had been kissing her tenderly and telling her he loved her. She shuddered at the memory. The experience with Sam had changed her. She was sceptical of people, perhaps even cynical. Ezra could easily be telling her one thing, and his girlfriend another. But, was she being unfair to Ezra to expect him to be a liar too? Maybe she was overthinking things, letting her past experiences cloud her judgement, and ruin her chances of happiness. Her head was spinning. Carla looked at her, and said simply, "Talk me through what you're thinking Chloe."

Taking a deep breath to steady herself, Chloe did her best not to let her voice waver as she spoke honestly. "I just don't want to get hurt again. Or, be the reason why someone else gets hurt."

Carla was nodding knowingly, chewing her sandwich. Somehow saying it all out loud made it so straightforward. The reason she didn't trust Ezra was because of Sam, and that wasn't fair. She was acting out of fear.

"It's just one big 'what if' situation at this point," Chloe said. "I want it to be true, I really do. But it just seems like, you know, it might not be."

Carla swallowed, and tilted her head, looking at Chloe caringly. "You need to start looking forward, instead of back." Chloe wasn't sure if she was referencing something, or being accidently profound, but her ears peaked. *What an excellent quote.* She dropped the last piece of her sandwich into her mouth. "If you ask me, the answer is simple. You need to meet this girlfriend. Find out if she really is on board."

Chloe nodded. Carla was right, that was the practical and logical solution. No use sitting here wondering and worrying when she knew what she wanted. A sudden determination filling her, she crammed the last of her sandwich into her mouth, and set off to find Ezra. She had to speak to him, and let him know that yes, she wanted to meet his girlfriend, and more importantly, she wanted to see him again.

Chapter 7

The path leading up to the front door of the light brick flat was overgrown with flowers. Ezra's car was parked in the driveway, and Chloe could hear music coming from inside through the open front window. It was a warm day, and Chloe had been feeling good this morning. She'd chosen a short black skater dress, which hit just above the knee, and a matching black cardigan. She had woken up before her alarm, had her morning cup of coffee, and even finished a load of laundry before she had to leave her place. She had agreed to meet Ezra and Avery at their place, and then head out to a nearby farmer's market to grab lunch. A completely friendly and non-threatening situation. But now, sitting in her car across the street, Chloe could barely breathe. It was all well and good researching, ruminating, and willing yourself to try new things, but actually doing it was another. Chloe was fast realising that she was way out of her comfort zone. But, if everything was as Ezra said it was, maybe this was the start of a brand new chapter for Chloe.

She stepped out of the car, picked up her bag and headed to the door. The floral smell of the garden was pleasantly overwhelming, as a few bees buzzed around, completely ignoring Chloe as her boots clicked on the concrete path. She reached the door, which was a faded wood, behind a standard flywire door. Taking a deep breath and reached for the doorbell. *Last chance to run*, she thought, and impulsively she hesitated. But, almost as fast as the thought came, she pushed it aside. She had made a decision to do what she wanted, not what she thought she should. Not let herself be controlled by fear. Isn't that what Carla said? Before she could second guess herself again, her finger was on the doorbell, and the classic tinny melody echoed through the house. With a clunk the door came unlocked, and then swung open to reveal Ezra. Chloe's heart skipped as the smell of his cologne hit her nose. There was something about his cologne that made her just melt, she couldn't explain it. He was wearing the same jeans as last Saturday, but now a more casual t-shirt. His hair was un-styled, falling to one side, and his beard unoiled and messy. There was something sexy about his unkemptness. He pushed his hair back as he broke out into a smile. "Wow Chloe," he gasped, looking her up and down. "You look…. great."

Chloe beamed, blushing a little. Ezra opened the screen door and stepped aside for her to enter, and she stepped onto the soft tan carpet of the living room. The walls were a dull white, a few framed pieces of art hung on the walls. The space was dominated by a dark grey an L-shaped sofa, decorated with a pastel pink faux fur throw and scatter cushions, the pink and red tones matching the floral curtains. A large square coffee table was in the centre of the room, facing a wall mounted TV, which had a music player open on the screen. Sunlight steamed through the large front facing window, covered by a sheer white curtain and framed by the two heavier, printed drapes. Although they were floral, they were modern, in a kind of Scandinavian way. The room smelt like vanilla, and Chloe spied several candles burning, as well as a bottle of wine and two glasses on the table. It had that feminine touch, and she was acutely aware she was now in Avery's home. It was not what she was expecting. Despite knowing she was coming to meet Avery, she had expected the space to me more masculine, more of Ezra's space.

Ezra closed the door behind him and placed a hand on Chloe's hip, gently stroking her ass over her skirt, guiding her to the couch. Her heart flipped. It was so subtle she wasn't sure if it was intentional or not, nevertheless, a tingle ran through her body as she remembered their moment in the car. When she had told Ezra she had decided she wanted to meet his girlfriend, his eyes had lit up. It was almost as if he has resigned himself to the fact that he had messed up with her, and she was never going to see him again. If only he knew how close he was to the truth. Shaking her head at his renewed boldness, she dropped her bag and sat down. She was so far out of her comfort zone she didn't know what to do with her hands, resting them on her knees.

"Sorry I'm not quite ready to go out yet." Ezra said, grabbing the bottle of wine and pouring her a generous glass. "Avery spent so long in the bathroom this morning I barely had a chance to get to the mirror."

"That's okay," Chloe managed to say, mind racing at a million miles an hour. She accepted the glass he offered to her and took a small sip. It was a very light sparkling wine, much too easy to drink. She didn't really know what else to say, she felt almost like she was in a dream. Being in another woman's space, with her boyfriend, it was just everything she had been taught was wrong. Everything that Sam had done to her, and she knew how much that hurt. But this time, it felt like she was the other woman, the niggling feeling of guilt stopping her from relaxing. *I don't know If I can do this.* She thought about what would happen if she just put her glass down and left. Reflexively she looked at the now closed door. She could leave, it's not like Ezra would stop her. But a large part of her really wanted to stay, despite her anxiety.

Ezra was sat on the chaise part of the couch, leaning back so that he was almost lying down. He was eyeing her curiously as he absent-mindedly swirled his wine. He was holding the glass awkwardly, obviously not a big wine drinker. "You okay?"

Chloe realised her entire body was tense, and made a conscious effort to relax her body, sinking back into the plush upholstery. She nodded, taking another sip of wine. "Yeah, it's just... weird for me."

Ezra nodded. "Me too. You're the first person I've actually had over."

Chloe's heart skipped a beat. *What?* Her face must have given away her thoughts, because Ezra continued. "Like I said the other night," he paused for a moment, a faraway expression on his face. Chloe too had a flash of memory back to the car, the passionate kissing, how his hands felt on her breasts, the thickness straining against his jeans. Ezra cleared his throat.
"I said this was new for us. We don't really want to let just anyone into our home. Or our lives."

"He thinks you're pretty special, Chloe." Chloe just about broke her neck looking towards the kitchen, where Avery had entered from. She was holding a tray of finger food, and gently shifted the wine over to fit it on the coffee table. She was a little taller than Chloe, with thick, dark hair, which she had braided over one shoulder. It fell like rope almost to her waist. She had skin the colour of cocoa, and smelt like coconut. She was wearing a long floral maxi dress, belted in to accentuate her waist. She was curvy too. *Ezra certainly has a type,* Chloe mused her herself. Avery sat next to Chloe, and she couldn't help but notice how her breasts were straining against the fabric of the dress. She was the most beautiful woman Chloe had ever seen. She was certainly not what Chloe had expected, although what she did actually expect, she had no idea.

Avery was pouring herself a drink, and Chloe's gaze snapped back to Ezra. He was eying the finger food, downed his wine and then leaned forward to grab some cheese and crackers.

"Uh, thank you." Chloe managed.

Avery met her gaze. Her eyes were like deep pools, and her expression hard to read. She exuded confidence. It was obvious that she was enjoying this very much. "It's okay Chloe. I know it's different, it goes against every relationship rule we're taught growing up." She topped up Chloe's glass as she spoke. "We really need to question who made those rules, you know?" She took a generous sip of wine.

Ezra smirked at Avery, and then turned to Chloe. "She has really found herself, come out of her shell. I'm proud of her."

Avery grinned, and said with a wink, "Yes, I even have a date tonight, so you two can be left alone."

Chloe placed her glass down on the table, laughing nervously. Avery was so warm, relaxed and stunningly beautiful, she made and Chloe felt her shoulders relaxing. She wasn't holding her arms quite so awkwardly anymore. Her voice was still caught in her throat, having no idea what to say. *What do you even talk about with the girlfriend of the guy you're seeing?* Chloe shook her head slightly, glancing at Avery, who was closing her lips around a spring roll. She made even that look sensual.

Sitting on the couch with her long, dark legs tucked beneath her, it truly struck Chloe how gorgeous Avery was. Her eyes were kind, and surrounded by long, dark lashes, accentuated by her lightly applied makeup. She had round, soft cheeks, but visible cheekbones which gave her a youthful and feminine appearance, currently covered with a light brush of golden highlighter.

Maybe it was the wine, but Chloe felt herself being unable to look away. "I, uh, really like your dress."

Avery broke out in a smile, "Thanks! I got it at an op shop. Only seven dollars, can you believe it?"

Chloe beamed, "I love op shopping!" That's something we can talk about. She felt herself relax. She was starting to feel silly for ever being nervous. Just then, Ezra stood and went to leave the room, shouting behind him, "I've got to get a better shirt on or we'll never leave, I'm hungry!"

There was a silence as Avery and Chloe were left alone for the first time. "Where do you go op shopping?" Avery continued, taking another sip of her wine. Without Ezra in the room, the tone had changed. "Over on Main Street." Chloe said flatly. Avery nodded as the conversation died. *Goddamn it Chloe*, she scolded, flushing with embarrassment as she met Avery's gaze, who was eyeing her kindly. "Chloe," Avery broke the silence, leaning back on the couch and unfolding her legs from underneath her. "Is there something on your mind?"

Chloe looked down at her knees, suddenly very aware of how pale they were. She didn't get much sun in the office. *Where do I even start?* She thought. *I have everything on my mind, all at once.*

"I guess," Chloe started, unsure of exactly how to put her thoughts into words. Her brain was a muddled mess. She took a deep breath, steading herself. "This is the first time I've ever done something like this," she explained. "My last relationship was a long one, seven years. It didn't end well." Her throat closed for a second, a sudden rush of emotion coming to her. She cleared her throat and shook her head to push it away. She was not about to cry now. Avery put her glass on the table, and leaned forward, placing her hand on Chloe's leg.

Chloe lifted her eyes to meet Avery's. They were deep and serious as she leant forward. Chloe could smell the soft herbal smell of her shampoo. "Nobody is about to hurt anyone here."

Avery squeezed her thigh slightly for emphasis, and Chloe felt a warmth flood over her. "We don't expect anything from you. Just honesty.

Honesty? Chloe thought, looking down at her knees. *How much honesty? Is keeping what happened with Sam to myself being dishonest?* She looked at Avery's warm eyes and gorgeous gentle smile. No, she couldn't bring herself to do it. *She'd probably lose respect for me,* Chloe thought. She took a breath, and forced a smile. She couldn't talk about it, not today at least.

She was three glasses of wine in when the trio finally left the house to walk to the market. Slightly tipsy, Chloe felt as if she was walking on air. The afternoon sun was soft and warm and her skin, and there was a gentle breeze. Avery was aggressively kind, and Chloe was feeling all of her apprehension and insecurities slowly melt away. There was nothing here but pure, open and honest love, and she could see no reason to not want to be part of that. For years she had walked around with blinkers on, afraid to even see another person as attractive in case Sam thought she was out of line. At the time, she had been flattered that Sam was so possessive of her, thinking it showed his love for her. She had crushed herself down for him. Now, she was beginning to see what real love was; honesty and trust. Avery was everything she wanted to be. Open, honest, unashamed to be herself. Plus, she was gorgeous.

Ezra grabbed her hand with a sweet smile, and led her though the crowd to a group of food trucks. Avery was trying to decide what to eat, chatting excitedly to Ezra and Chloe. She was beaming, obviously in her element, as Ezra leaned in to speak to her, putting his face close to her ear and hand gently on her lower back, then, he moved to Chloe to do the same. They were in public, and not at all trying to hide that they were romantically involved with each other. Chloe felt the wonderful and excited, natural feelings one has at the beginning of a relationship. A freedom from rules and restrictions which, in the past, had only served to make her smaller.

They grabbed a seat at a round table, setting out their food in front of them. Ezra sat between Avery and Chloe, and was beaming from ear to ear. Laying out the plates on the table, they had an eclectic spread of dumplings, chips smothered in gravy, and nachos. Avery was first to dive in, swooping a dumpling off the plate before Ezra even had time to pick up a fork, and placing it between her lips with a devilish smirk. "Oh my god, Chloe, these are amazing, you have to try one!"
Chloe responded by reaching across to pick one up, but fumbled with her chopsticks. Eventually, she managed to pick one up, but at this point the trio were giggling. Trying to bite through a dumpling mid-laugh, Chloe spilled sauce down her face, and attempted to catch it with her free hand.

Ezra reached over to wipe her face for her with a napkin, still laughing, and Chloe felt that familiar wave of electric attraction.

There was still a slight tinge of guilt she was feeling, being so attracted to Ezra, and right in front of his girlfriend, but with each little moment that was fading away.

It was only a three block walk back, but as the trio came up to the house, Avery bounded ahead of the group, towards the door. Slipping her key in, she looked back at Ezra and Chloe with a playful and exaggerated hair flick. "I am *dying* for some more wine!"

"We're out of wine, I think," Ezra offered, as Avery disappeared into the house. Ezra held the door for Chloe, and she entered, feeling a soft tap to her rear as she passed him. She heard him chuckle, and could hear the arousal in it. Her heart jumped, realising she was probably going to end up in bed with him before she left this house again. The very thought of it excited her, and she could feel the soft tingle between her legs.

"Gin it is then!" Avery's voice echoed from the kitchen. "You like gin, right Chloe?"

"Only with lime," she replied, stepping into the space and hearing Ezra close the door behind them. She stepped towards the kitchen to help, but Ezra grabbed her hand, pulling her close to him. She was wearing flat shoes, so, chest to chest, he was about a head taller than her. He made her feel tiny and delicate as he twisted his fingers into hers, and cupped the back of her head with his spare hand. Her heart flipped. He was about to kiss her, with Avery right in the next room. There was a small part of her that felt like this was wrong, but that part was fast being drowned by her raw attraction for Ezra. He pulled her closer, and she rose up on to her tiptoes to meet him for the kiss.

His lips were soft, and the kiss gentle, at first. Ezra made a small, excited noise, and pushed deeper into the kiss. As his tongue entered her mouth, Chloe felt a wave of excitement run through her, and a tiny moan escaped her lips.

The sound of Avery placing Chloe's drink on the table caused her to jump. She turned, and was half expecting to see Avery standing there angrily. Instead, Avery was smiling, and sitting herself down on the couch with a relaxed flop. "Don't let me stop you," she said, cheerfully. "Callum will be here any minute to pick me up anyway."

Chloe's heart was pounding, and her face flushed, but she stepped away from Ezra to join Avery on the couch. As she sat down, she looked back at him. He was still watching her, one hand on the growing bulge in his jeans, trying to hide his arousal. He turned away when he realised that she had seen him, and strode towards the kitchen. "I'll just get myself a whiskey."
"You do that," Avery replied, smirking knowingly to herself as she sipped her gin. Chloe was overwhelmed, she had never felt so welcome, nor been in such an open and honest space before. She picked up her glass, and took a deep swig. Avery was the only other person in the room, but right now it felt a little awkward to be looking in her direction. If Chloe was being honest, she'd been slightly aroused by that kiss. Chloe instead was diverting her gaze to their bookshelf, which was full to the brim with books of all sorts. Her eyes skimmed the spines without taking in any titles.

Suddenly, Chloe felt a hand on her knee. Looking over, she saw Avery, levelling her with a serious face. "It's okay," she reassured her with a smile. Chloe was certain that she saw Avery glance at her up and down, but it was so quick she was sure she had imagined it. Chloe opened her mouth to thank her for being so kind and accepting of her, but before she could there was a knock on the door. Avery jumped up, downing the rest of her gin in one gulp, and bounded towards the door. Swinging it open, Chloe got a glance at the person she could only assume was Callum. He was a similar build to Ezra, but with long, light brown hair tied into a ponytail, and a beard that hit his chest. *I guess Avery has a type too.*

Ezra entered back into the room with his whiskey, and nodded towards the door. "Hey, man."

"Hey dude," Callum replied, in a smooth, rumbling voice. He then directed his gaze to Avery. "You ready?"

"Yep!" she chirped, grabbing her bag and bouncing out the door. "You two have fun!"
She shut the heavy wooden door behind her, and Chloe looked up at Ezra, who was now standing awkwardly in the doorway to the kitchen, holding his whiskey.

They were alone.

Chapter 8

There was a stillness as the two of them looked at each other.
Neither spoke or moved for a long moment. Ezra raised his whiskey
to his mouth wordlessly, taking a deep sip of the caramel liquid. He
lowered his eyes to the floor, almost as if he needed to remind
himself where he was. Suddenly Chloe became aware that she had
been staring and a flush came over her face, as she turned back
towards the table, and her barely touched gin. She took a sip,
savouring the taste. She heard Ezra's glass connect softly with the
kitchen counter, and then his footsteps as he walked toward her.
She was suddenly self-conscious about how she was sitting, about
whether her hair was lying flat, and ran her fingers through it
nervously to fix it. All the while, avoiding looking at him. She could
feel him standing close to her, she could see his feet, bare now on
the tan carpet. Still, she felt that, in order to keep breathing, she
couldn't look at him. She was hyper aware of her surroundings; the
soft movement of the sheer curtains from the breeze, the syrupy
vanilla smell from the candles they'd re-lit, the engraved texture on
the gin glass beneath her fingers. Her breath caught in her chest as
she felt Ezra lower himself on to the couch next to her. With Avery
gone it was suddenly very intimate, very real that he was there with
her. He put his hand on her knee and she froze, her heart pounding.

"Chloe," his deep voice was barely a whisper as he said her name,
and she looked up at him. His face was soft, a tender expression. In
that moment, all she could think was that his eyes were beautiful,
and she couldn't for the life of her think of anything to say. His hand
reached for her chin, his fingers guiding her face towards his. She
was spellbound, helpless, falling into the kiss.
His lips were soft against hers, and tasted of whiskey. Unlike the
time in the car, this kiss was soft. She placed her glass on the table

with a soft thud, but it sounded a million miles away. She was wrapped in his warmth, his cologne. She could feel the soft fabric of his shirt as she moved her hands over his back. His hand moved to her hair, gently running across her scalp, and then gently, but purposefully, grabbing her hair to pull her head backwards.

She couldn't help but let out a small gasp, his kisses moving to her neck. Her chest rose to meet him, waves of arousal flowing through her body. She was opening up, like a rose. All of her insecurities and fears had been soothed, and she was allowing herself to relax for the first time in a long time.

One of his hands was in her hair and the other on her waist, slowly sliding slowly downwards to her thigh. He pulled back from the kiss, and stared at her for a moment, his eyes intense. Her stomach flipped. She looked him in the eyes, but had nothing to say. She had seen the bulge in his jeans before, and the image of it was all she could think of. Right now, she wanted him to fuck her, and nothing else mattered.

With one hand he moved her hips gently, but effortlessly, so one of her legs was now on the couch. He positioned himself to face her, between her legs now, and came up for a second kiss. Her breathing heavy, she ran her hand up his chest, over the soft fabric of his shirt. She could feel his weight on her, her chest pressing against his, as she fell gently back onto the scatter cushions, and the arm of the couch behind them. She felt her hair pile softly around her head, tickling her cheeks, and she moved her hand to his arm as she lay back. His skin was warm under her fingers, the muscle in his forearm tense as it supported him. His other hand was lower down, sliding slowly up her thigh, under the hem of her skirt. The roughness of his fingers tickled the soft skin, untouched for so long. She breathed in sharply as a ripple of arousal ran through her, her chest straining against the fabric of her dress as she held her breath. She could feel her skin vibrating as she pushed herself up with one arm to meet his kiss. It started soft, but as Chloe's heart began to race, she pushed her lips into his, and he pushed back, the kiss becoming less controlled. His beard tickled her chin as his tongue expertly explored the inside of her mouth. A soft moan escaped from her lips and he pulled back, slowing the kiss. She smiled, and leant in, planting a gentle peck on his mouth. He smiled, his eyes warm and inviting as he gazed at her.

With a shiver and a sharp inhale of surprise, she felt his thumb reach her underwear, and immediately she longed for more. Chloe felt his hot breath on her neck, the fabric of his shirt against her arms. More than anything she wanted to tear it off of him right now. Pushing her hips towards his hand as they kissed, she felt him tense up slightly, as he lifted his lips back from hers and gave a little chuckle. Ezra gently stroked the outside of her underwear with his thumb, just enough to tease her. She inhaled sharply, her eyes wild with desire as she looked at him, practically on top of her now, his hair falling forward over his face. He was smiling, enjoying her arousal thoroughly. She could feel his cock against her hip, still trapped in his jeans, its thickness straining against the fabric. The thought of it inside her was almost too much, and she felt herself growing wet, the warm juices soaking the thin fabric.

Almost effortlessly, he moved her underwear aside with his fingers, and gently traced his fingers up her opening, feeling the wetness. She saw his eyes widen, and he groaned slightly, as he gathered some of her juice on his fingertips and began to massage her clit. His fingers made her shudder with arousal, the arm she was using to support herself quivering underneath her. He sat back between her legs, his full focus on her. She had begun to breathe heavily, and rapidly, the stimulation on her clitoris bringing her close. She was aching to free herself from her clothes, and she struggled, rushing to pull her arms free from the top of her dress, exposing her bra and the fullness of her breasts.

"Can I... enter you?" Ezra growled, and Chloe buzzed with excitement. Nobody had ever *asked* like that before, and it was so incredibly sexy. She nodded, biting her lip. Ezra groaned, and slid two fingers easily inside her, his thumb still drawing circles. Chloe was swimming in her own sea of arousal, her body involuntarily writhing as he inserted his fingers. She was whimpering, about to reach orgasm, as she sunk back into the cushions. She grabbed at one of her breasts roughly, riding the wave of ecstasy. Her breath caught in her throat as she came, her body pulsing rhythmically, and a deep moan escaping her lips. She could hear Ezra moaning softly to himself, enjoying watching her writhe with pleasure. Eyes closed and her head swimming, she no longer had any thoughts that this could be in any way wrong. No more thoughts of the past or worries for the future spun in her mind. Instead, she was simply present, in the moment, lost in the sensations of his expert touch. The fog of ecstasy only lasted a moment, however, and soon she was returning to the soft couch, the smell of vanilla candles, and Ezra. Coming down from the high of the orgasm, the first she had had in so long, she opened her eyes and looked at Ezra. He had one hand gently stroking the outside of her pussy, the other absent-mindedly stroking the tip of his cock through his jeans. His eyes were wide, and he noticed her looking at him, still panting heavily from the orgasm.

"I've never seen a woman cum like that." He said, blinking. "You came so hard I could feel it gripping my fingers."
Her mind was still distant, and words were not coming back to her very quickly. So, she just nodded. After a moment, she swallowed, laughing a little, still a bit high from such an intense orgasm.

Sitting up, she pulled her dress off over her head, and reached back to unclip her bra. As her breasts fell freely, she heard Ezra grunt. Looking at him, he seemed spellbound by her, his hand still absently rubbing his cock through his jeans. She moved over towards him, lifting his shirt over his head to reveal an almost hairless chest. He was obviously strong, but his skin was soft to touch. She kissed him, deeply, as she slid her hand down towards his belt. She was not about to wait a moment longer to see him naked. Now she was the one hungry for it.

Undoing his belt, she felt him shift his hips towards her. He had moved his hand away, and was allowing her to take control now. From the way he was moving, she could tell he wanted her to take it out for him. With the buttons undone and the fly of his jeans open, his cock pushed outwards, still contained in his underwear. She slipped his jeans down as he lifted his hips, his penis pulsing with excitement. Looking at his face, she thought his expression was a combination of arousal and awe.

Suddenly feeling very powerful, she stood in front of him, naked except for her black underwear. His mouth was open, and he bit his lip as he reached for her hand, pulling it towards his crotch. She knelt down on the floor, and gently stroked her fingers over the length of his shaft, over his underwear. He grunted, and his penis pulsed against her hand. She slipped her fingers beneath the waistband, purposefully taking her time, and pulled his cotton boxers down to expose his rock-hard shaft. It was a good seven inches, curved slightly upward, and just a little too thick for Chloe to wrap her hand around entirely. His back arched with pleasure as she took hold of it, the tip glistening with a small amount of precum.

Gently stroking it, right in front of her eyes, was a huge turn on for Chloe. It had been a long time since she had held a penis, and never one this thick. Seeing it there, rock hard in her hands, and knowing it was because of her, made her feel incredible. Any doubts she had about her appearance, any niggling anxiety about her awkwardness was forgotten. She felt in control, and that felt so good. She could hear Ezra softly melting into the pleasure of it, his breathing becoming heavier and deeper. As she slid her hand up and down the length of it, it throbbed beneath her fingers, fuelling her own arousal. Looking at his face, he had his eyes closed, and his mouth curled into a content smile, but slightly open. Chloe began moving her body closer to his cock, between Ezra's legs, the soft skin of her breast touched his thigh. He inhaled sharply, his dick straining, and his eyes sprung open to look at her. Topless, between his knees, her plump breasts only inches from his cock. Her long, black hair was falling about her face, slightly dishevelled, giving her a wild look. In that moment, his face was twisted, as if he was fighting every urge to grab her by the back of the head and ram his cock into her mouth. The thought of that, of him being completely at her mercy in this moment, sent a thrill through her. He put his hands behind his head, and Chloe thought, with a rush of excitement, to hold himself back. With a devilish grin, Chloe leaned forward towards his cock, and for a moment Ezra seemed frozen. Her lips parted and she stuck out her tongue, intentionally slow, maintaining eye contact as she delicately licked the length of his shaft.

Ezra moaned loudly, uncontrollably, as Chloe tasted the slightly salty flavour of the delicate skin. His moan sent a rush of arousal through her, and she opened her mouth, closing her soft pink lips gently around the tip, sucking gently. She closed her eyes, playing with the tip with her tongue, before slowly sliding the length of it into her mouth. Ezra writhed with pleasure, whispering softly, "fuck!" Chloe, confident in her skills, although admittedly a bit out of practise, thoroughly enjoyed giving blowjobs, because of reactions like that. She smiled to herself, pleased that she could just about fit the whole thing in, but not quite, and she struggled to stifle a gag as it hit the back of her throat. Ezra was quietly moaning, as she used both her hand and mouth together on his cock. She could feel his cock growing even harder and thicker between her lips, which sent a shiver of pleasure through her. She was so aroused by Ezra's soft moans, steadily getting less controlled, she couldn't resist slipping her free hand into her underwear, feeling her own wetness with her fingers.

Ezra's hand was in her hair now and he was guiding her steadily up and down the length of him. He was not holding back his enjoyment now, with gasps of "Oh yeah" and "Fuck" escaping his lips between his heavy breaths. Chloe was almost out of her body with arousal, between the ultimate turn on of his penis in her mouth, his hand gripping her hair, and her rubbing herself, she couldn't hold back her own moans and gasps of pleasure. She could feel the texture of the tan carpet digging into her knees, as the swell of the impending orgasm began to fill her body. Ezra moved his second hand to her hair now, and held her head still, instead using his hips to thrust into her mouth. Her eyes were watering, and a small amount of saliva fell from the corner of her mouth as she looked up at him, sweaty and dishevelled, and met his gaze. His eyes widened, and he let out a deep growling moan. "Aw fuck Chloe," he said, his breath catching in his chest. He didn't have to say it, but she knew he was on the verge of cumming. Which was good, really, as his unrelenting thrusts were starting to make her jaw ache. The rhythm of his thrusts faltered, and Chloe whimpered a moan, his pleasure driving her closer to the edge herself, although his enthusiasm was making it difficult for her to keep her own rhythm. With one loud, unbridled groan, her mouth began to fill with his juices, the sour taste overwhelming her mouth. She had to use both her hands to stabilise herself, abandoning her tingling clit, but managed to hold the liquid in as his thrusts and moans slowed. With a few final, slow licks, she delicately removed her mouth from his pulsing cock, sat back on her knees, and swallowed deliberately.

Ezra had laid his head back as he came, and, panting, he was still for a moment. With a small grunt, he raised his head, using one hand to wipe the sweat from his brow, and looked directly at Chloe. He watched her, still kneeling on the floor in front of him, as she swallowed his load, wiping the stray spit and cum from her chin with the back of her hand.

Her nipples rock hard, and as his gaze took in her body, her underwear was soaked through. After a few breaths, he was able to string together a sentence. "You really like sucking cock, don't you?"

Chloe looked at him mischievously, arousal still pulsing through her body. She grinned at him playfully as she replied, "I really do."

She stood up, ready to find her clothes and get herself together. She was keen to finish herself off, but since Ezra had come already, she was assuming the sex was over. Ezra pulled his boxer briefs up, putting his slowly softening cock away, and stood to be next to her, pushing his jeans off in the process. He stepped behind her, his body warm against hers, his big hands gripping her breasts from behind, causing her to gasp again. He slipped his hands to her hips, and slid her underwear down to her thighs, before reaching on hand between to touch her again. "Holy fuck," he muttered. "You really are wet."

She managed a nod, as he began to massage her clitoris again, slowly. She was so aroused already, it hardly seemed fair for him to tease her like this. She moaned gently, and pushed herself against him, her hips moving against his hand, her body ready for another orgasm. She was impatient for it. Before she knew it, he had used both his hands to turn her to face him, and gently push her back onto the couch. Chloe looked up at him as she fell back into the cushions, his eyes glistening with desire. They were both still for a moment as he took in the sight of her, naked and sweaty on the couch, her hair a mess, and probably her makeup too. In that moment, she couldn't have cared less about her hair or makeup. She felt beautiful, sensual, and desired. He used both hands to slide her underwear completely off, maintaining eye contact, which caused her to gasp with excitement. He knelt in front of her, and moved both of his hands to part her thighs, somehow both forcefully and gently. The pressure of his fingers on her skin was exhilarating. She knew what was coming, and found herself holding her breath with anticipation. Meeting her eyes for a moment, he smiled. "Can I eat you out?" His baritone voice causing her to tremble with anticipation.

She exhaled, smiling "Please."

He moved his face downwards, disappearing between her thighs, and she closed her eyes as she felt his soft lips touch her clitoris. A wave of pleasure rippled through her as he began to move his tongue over it, a combination of licks and circles causing her to begin moaning uncontrollably. It had been a long time since she had been intimate with anyone, but even longer since anyone had gone down on her, and never before like this. Ezra seemed to know exactly what he was doing between her thighs. Before long she was at her peak again, thighs spasming against his shoulders, gasping for air as she came, her body pulsating with pleasure.

Ezra moaned from between her legs, feeling her orgasm beneath him, but, to Chloe's surprise, did not stop. If anything, it seemed to make him more enthusiastic, as he used his broad tongue to lick the opening of her vagina, almost drinking her juices. She felt powerful, almost dominant, with his face in her crotch and, looking down at him enjoying the taste of her, she could not help but place her hand in his hair, guiding his head into her, she same way he had done to her only minutes before. He grunted between her thighs, enjoying her taking control, and continued to pleasure her with his mouth. Within moments she could feel another orgasm building, but this was different, more intense. She was losing control of herself, her moans becoming louder and more primal as the pleasure built. Ezra lifted his head for just a moment, looking at her face, as he placed two fingers at her opening. He watched her face with unrestrained enjoyment as she inhaled, tilting her hips towards his fingers eagerly, and he waited for just a moment there. Impatiently she moaned in protest, and his smile turned mischievous as his fingers entered her. She gasped, a rush of pleasure washing over her, as she felt him find her g-spot. Her stomach turned as the pleasure built deep inside her, and her breathing became deeper and slower. She closed her eyes, riding this intoxicating wave of pleasure. She almost jumped as she again felt Ezra's tongue on her clitoris, the combination of the two sending her almost immediately to the peak of her arousal. She had never in her life experienced something as intense as this, and she felt herself losing control entirely, falling into the sensation. She fell back on the cushions, her moans becoming deep groans, as she felt her body tensing. Ezra felt it too, and increased the intensity of his caressing and licking, which sent her over the edge. Her entire body was shuddering, her thighs pushing open, her back arched. She couldn't breathe, she felt like she was floating outside of her body. Ezra, from between her legs, was moaning in pleasure as he pushed his face against her.

He pulled back, and looked down at Chloe, who was struggling to catch her breath. His beard was dripping with her juices, and he attempted to wipe it off with a satisfied grin. *That is a sight I am going to remember for a long time,* Chloe noted with satisfaction. Chloe adjusted herself on the couch, and noticed a large, wet puddle between her legs. "Holy fuck," she whispered, more amazed than embarrassed. Her arms were shaking, her body weak from the intensity of her most recent orgasm, and she let herself sink back into the soft cushions for another moment. In the afterglow, she felt amazing, like she had zero worries in the world. She had almost forgotten how amazing it felt to have good sex. Ezra noticed the puddle too, as he stood up, and chuckled to himself, pushing his hair back from his face. "Oh man, I'm going to have to flip the cushion or something."

Chloe smiled, still attempting to catch her breath. She watched as Ezra stood, picking up her almost-empty glass, and gestured with it towards her. "Another one?"

Chloe nodded, smiling, still unable to quite form words. With a satisfied laugh, Ezra left the room, and she was alone. Naked and happy, she wouldn't want it any other way.

Chapter 9

It was dead on 4pm the next Friday, and Chloe was clocking off for the week, ready to head to a small work function some of the staff from marketing had arranged. She had managed to sneak away from her desk a bit early to get changed, and was already wearing her skinny jeans, ankle boots, and a plain white, oversized shirt. She had a denim jacket hung over her arm, ready for the cooler evening air which was sure to arrive soon. Waiting for the lift to leave the building, she reached up to undo her hair, letting her midnight black locks fall freely about her shoulders. It felt good to run her hand through her hair, ruffling the wavy mess into a somewhat presentable style. The doors opened, and she stepped inside the empty carriage, the mirror on the rear reflecting her image back to her. She looked good. In fact, she had felt amazing since her date with Ezra the weekend before. She really was letting go of her past and allowing herself to just have fun. Dating as an adult was incredibly different to dating as a teen. There was no longer a prerequisite of love, no promises of a future, in order to be able to enjoy each other physically. And she definitely enjoyed him physically.

A quiet thud made her jump out of her reverie, and she saw Ezra, in the mirror, catching the slowly closing door with his hand. It opened again to allow him to enter, looking Chloe up and down. They had been friendly at work the whole week, attempting to mask their attraction for each other with casual and friendly conversation, sneaking lustful glances at each other right under the noses of their unsuspecting co-workers. In a planning meeting the previous day, Ezra had sat down next to Chloe, making her heart jump into her chest, and proceeded to casually stroke her thigh beneath the desk the entire time. It made Chloe excited to have such a scandalous secret. In fact, keeping it secret was almost half the fun. The doors closed on the lift and she stood there in silence, alone with Ezra for the first time since they had had sex on his couch the week before. Memories of that day came flooding back to her, especially the sight of him smiling with her juices in his beard, and her body was aching to experience it again. She had deprived herself from the sexual touch of another for so long, that she only how was realising what she had been missing out on. And she was finding herself eager to make up for lost time.

"You look amazing in those jeans," he said finally, his eyes unapologetically on her backside.

"Thank you," she managed with a flirtatious smile. He was wearing his same jeans, with a short sleeve button down shirt. In the small space she was overwhelmed by the smell of his cologne, obviously freshly applied to go out. It was like a spell on her, the smell alone making her tingle with arousal. He leaned in to her, and spoke quietly, his mouth curling into that familiar mischievous grin. "I plan on fucking you tonight."

Her eyes widened at the idea, and her face flushed, but she loved it. It was incredible to feel so desired. She looked up at him, but before she could speak the doors to the lift opened, and he stepped out, still grinning. "See you at the bar!"

It was only a short drive away, chosen because of its proximity to their work, and the entire drive there, alone in her car, Chloe was wishing she was instead driving home so she could be alone with Ezra. Where her thoughts not long ago had been consumed with the tragedy of her breakup with Sam, now her ruminations were about Ezra. As she pulled into the parking lot, she was able to centre herself. She had made her life about a man before, but she was not about to give up her social life for anyone ever again. *No man worth my time would ever ask me to*, she reminded herself firmly. She was ready to have a few drinks with her friends. As good as sex was with Ezra, it could wait.

She entered the bar confidently, and she saw her colleagues sitting in the outdoor area. Ezra was already there, deep in conversation with the other men from the Logistics department, pint in hand. He looked in her direction as she walked by, and she smiled to herself. It felt amazing to be wanted by someone physically, especially after so long. She headed to the bar to get herself a drink, deciding on a glass of prosecco after a quick glace of the wine list.

As she returned to the table, glass of bubbles in hand, she found herself a seat next to Carla, opposite Ezra. She joined in the conversation, keen to enjoy the social event, even though her body was impatiently aching for Ezra's touch. Despite her best intentions, she found herself glancing over at him frequently. Likewise, she felt his eyes on her often, and she was enjoying being the object of his lust. She found herself very conscious of her own body; how she was sitting, how her hair was falling, the expression she had on her face. She had taken her time drinking her glass, and was playing absent-mindedly with the stem as it sat on the table, empty. She was half listening to the conversation, enjoying the atmosphere of the bar, when she heard something that made her heart stop.

"So, I was listening to a podcast yesterday," Travis was saying to the group. "They were talking about this new relationship style, polyamory? Where you date multiple people at the same time."

"Ew," said Lauren, another one of her colleagues. Lauren was slightly older than Chloe, an athletic bleach blonde. She was never one to shy away from sharing her opinion. "Sounds like an excuse to cheat if you ask me."

"That's the thing," Travis said, unbothered. "It's not cheating. Everyone knows who you are dating, it's all above board." He took a sip of his drink. "I don't know, the way they talked about it... it kind of made sense."

Carla nodded, looking pointedly at Lauren. "Yeah, my cousin does that."

"That's disgusting," Lauren practically spat. She was halfway through a bottle of red wine and had the enthusiasm you would expect. "I would never let another woman touch my man! If my man even *looks* at another woman, he owes me an apology." She turned to Chloe, gesturing at her with her glass, "your boyfriend cheated on you, back me up here Chloe."

Chloe's eyes went wide, and she glanced over at Ezra unconsciously. *Shit*, she scolded herself, looking away nervously. Ezra was listening to this entire conversation, smirking. "Cheating is really shitty." She said carefully, but then added with a shrug. "But come on Lauren, you can't be so harsh about how other people want to live their lives."

Lauren scoffed, filling her glass from her bottle. "At least none of you are doing something like that."
Carla gave Chloe a knowing look, with a cheeky smile. There was a moment of silence in the group as Travis glared at Laura, who was oblivious, doing her best to make it to the bottom of her glass.

"So, Chloe," Carla said from the seat next to her, nudging her shoulder playfully. "How's your love life going? You still haven't old me anything about this new guy you've been seeing!"

Chloe laughed nervously, as all eyes turned to her expectantly. Most of the group had left by this point, only staying for one polite drink and leaving. There was seven of them left now, all of whom Chloe had decent work friendship with. Lauren turned to face her excitedly, eyes wide. "Chloe! You didn't tell us you were seeing someone!"

No, Lauren, I didn't tell you because you'd shout it from the rooftops! She thought, annoyed. She shook her head and chose her words carefully. "Yeah, well," Chloe started, not really knowing how much to say. She was very suddenly the centre of attention in the small group. She shuffled in her seat, desperately trying to not look over at Ezra. Please, nobody put two and two together. "It's still a pretty new thing, you know."

Carla leaned over to her with a smug, tipsy grin. "Did you fuck him yet though?"

Chloe couldn't help herself. She giggled coyly, and shrugged. Carla erupted into cheers, becoming a little too loud. "You did! You dirty bitch!"

Chloe was trying to shush her friend through her laughter, which was mostly directed at Carla's outlandish behaviour. She noticed the three remaining members of the Logistics team were now looking at her with raised eyebrows. Ezra was leaning back in his chair, a smirk creeping over his lips.

"You finally get laid?" Luke, another one of them asked, joining the conversation.

"Oh my god," Chloe said, running her hand through her hair in embarrassment. "It's not that big of a deal."

"Um, yeah it is." Carla said. "You finally broke the drought after your loser ex. What was it, ten months? Eleven?"

"Shut-up!" Chloe said, glaring daggers at Carla. Carla was tipsy, and looking smugly at Chloe, as she picked up her pint glass and slid the last mouthful into her open lips. She popped her empty glass on the table. "Must have been some decent dick if you're being so shy about it."

Chloe gawked at her, and Ezra stifled a laugh. "Carla!" she said, picking up her glass, but finding it empty. Rolling her eyes at her immature friend, she stood up. "I think I need a drink."

Leaning on the bar, Chloe was doing her best to stay annoyed at her friend's behaviour, but the truth was that it didn't really bother her that much at all. While the Chloe of a few months ago would have been mortified talking about her sex life in public, today, Chloe was finding that she was struggling to find even a shred of embarrassment. In a short space of time she was able to see she was more than just Sam's ex. She was a grown woman who was in control of her own life. She still didn't want to become the next office scandal, and was content to keep her cards close to her chest.

"Prosecco please," she said, smiling at the bartender. As he turned to the fridge, she felt a hand slide softly across her backside. Glancing to her left in surprise she saw Ezra, a look of amusement painted on his face. She raised her eyebrows at him. "Hey, what if someone saw?"

"You mean what if Laura saw?" he said, raising his eyebrows as he leaned on the bad. "She's half plastered anyway, she wouldn't notice if she was looking directly at us." Chloe shrugged, and turned back to accept her drink from the bartender.

"Hey," he said, stopping her from leaving. He ordered his drink quickly, and then turned back to her. "You never told me your last boyfriend cheated on you."

"Does it matter?" She sighed, looking him in the eyes. He was searching her face, trying to read something in her expression, but she was doing everything in her power to hold it together. Inside, it felt like she had been punched in the chest. *Why am I so pathetic?* She scolded herself. *This is why he did it, Chloe. Because you're u sad and sorry loser.* She grimaced, shaking her head to get the awful internal monologue to stop. No, she was not a loser, she was a sexy, intelligent woman. She took a deep breath, attempting to use a grounding technique she used in therapy.

"Chloe," he looked at her, concerned. "It matters if it's affecting how you feel about our… situation."

"Ezra." She said, purposefully. "I dated a guy for seven years and he cheated on me. At the time, I thought he was great, but looking back I see that he was awful; the whole relationship was full of red flags." The words poured out, no doubted aided by the wine she had been drinking. She took a sip of her drink, trying to suppress the emotion that was welling up inside of her. She could recite it now like it wasn't a problem, she knew the facts. Sam was an asshole. She knew it all, and yet she still wanted to go back to the way she was before her world fell apart. She wanted to go back to seeing her life spread out before her, a series of milestones in the relationship escalator she would share with her partner. Marriage, a house, children. *Now I'll never get those things* she thought sourly. Even as she thought them, she knew they weren't necessarily true. She could meet someone else and have it all.

But that wasn't really what she was upset about. No, she was angry that she had been lied to, and that she had been stupid enough to think that Sam was telling her the truth. She never got to have a wild birthday party, make out with strangers in a bar, have one night stands... *I never even got to go to parties at my uni,* she mused angrily. Sam didn't allow it, although she let him go to his parties without her. She could feel tears growing in her eyes, realising how much of her life she had wasted on this guy. "I missed out on a lot. I am so sick of shrinking myself down for people. I just want a chance to be *me*."

But that wasn't really it either. The core of her anger was about *that night* when she had found out he had been cheating. She was so embarrassed about how she had acted. About letting herself get into that position. *If he knew,* she thought, looking up at Ezra's face. *If he knew what had happened, what a crazy bitch I was, what I let him do... He'd drop me in a heartbeat too.*

His eyebrows were raised as he took his pint from the bartender. He met her gaze. "What else?"

Chloe hesitated. Maybe she could tell him? *No.* She scolded herself, pulling her lips tight and shaking her head. Concern suddenly flashed across Ezra's face. "Chloe?"

"Nothing," She said curtly. She could tell from his face he didn't believe her. Inside, she was raging. *When am I going to stop being so upset whenever anyone mentions him?*

"Chloe-" he started, and she cut him off.

"Drop it, Ezra." she said, more firmly than she meant to. There was a moment of silence before she whispered. "I'm sorry."

Ezra shrugged, seeming unbothered. "Want to get out of here?"

She shrugged, taking another sip of her drink coyly. She could use a distraction from her feelings. And, she felt like she needed to make up to Ezra for being so short with him. "Maybe we can actually make it back to my place this time?"

Chapter 10

Attempting to not arouse the suspicion of her co-workers, Chloe had left the bar before Ezra, and so had arrived at her place first. Parking her small car in her designated place, she was becoming aware of the butterflies in her stomach. Walking quickly to her door, she slipped her key in with ease and entered into her newly renovated kitchen. She had ripped out the dated one only a few weeks prior, and replaced it with a much more modern one. Her main room was open plan, but not very spacious, and her sofa and TV took up most of the rest of the space. She flicked on the lights, and headed into her bedroom, quickly arranging the decorative cushions on the king size bed she mostly left stacked on the floor, until company came over. It occurred to her then that had been some time that anyone had visited her in this place, even a friend. With that complete, she let out a sigh, and stood with her hands on her hips. Ezra was on his way over, with the sole intention to have sex with her. She had never experienced this before, somebody just wanting her sexually, with no conditions attached. Chloe looked over at the wardrobe with floor to ceiling, mirrored sliding doors. She smiled at her reflection. Chloe had spent so long focusing on what had happened to her, that she hadn't realised that she had become almost obsessed with it, had let it define her. Right now, she felt like a completely different woman than she was months ago. Her head was held higher, she was smiling more. She felt powerful, and she liked it.

Just then there was a knock at the door and she almost jumped out of her skin. She took a deep breath before walking calmly to let Ezra in. He was standing leaning against the doorframe as she opened the door, staring back towards the road. Casually, he tilted his head to look at her.

"Hey hot stuff," He said playfully. Chloe could see his eyes wandering over her body like a hungry lion. She smiled, a rush of excitement running through her, and stepped back to let him in to her space. He stood in the centre of the kitchen, looking around and nodding in approval, the kitchen suddenly feeling much smaller with his broad frame in it. "Nice place."

"Thanks," she replied, shutting the door behind him. In two strong steps he was behind her, lips on her neck. The force of it caused her to fall forward onto the door, her breasts and arms hitting the hard wood, and she let out a small squeak of surprise. His kiss sent a shiver through her, and his broad hands were making their way over her body, drinking in her curves. Ezra made a small grunt of enthusiasm, and grabbed one of her arms forcefully, spinning her around.

He was kissing her deeply and passionately, pushing her back against the door, his body leaning into hers. His hands wandered from her hips to her chest, Ezra moaning softly with arousal as he gripped her soft, supple breasts over her clothing. He smelt like beer and cologne, and she couldn't get enough of it. His excitement triggering hers, Chloe lifted her lips from his, biting her bottom lip as she felt herself getting moist. Her hips pushed forward, eager for his touch, and he responded with a groan, hands moving swiftly from her breasts to her jeans. His kisses stopping for a moment, he unfastened and pulled her jeans down to her boots, revealing her plain black underwear. His hands worked back around her hips as his kissing resumed, moving again from her neck back to her mouth. He pressed his hips against hers as his hands cupped her butt, a

slight moan escaping his mouth as her squeezed her cheeks. She
could feel him getting hard against her hip, and she whimpered
softly, overcome with excitement.

He pulled his hips back slightly to allow one of his hands to slip
between her legs, one finger finding its way expertly past her
underwear and slipping between her juicy lips. She gasped as she
felt his touch, and he grunted with excitement as he felt how wet
she was for him. Before she could think, he had inserted two fingers
into her, causing her to inhale sharply with pleasure. He began
massaging her g-spot, causing ripples of pleasure to radiate through
her. He levelled her with a steady gaze, her back leaning against the
door as she shuddered and whimpered. She was helpless in that
moment, completely at his mercy, and she liked it. It must have
been written all over her face, because he slowed his fingering, a
mischievous smirk crossing his lips. He slipped his fingers out of her,
gently caressing the length of her moistness. "Can I pull your hair?"
he asked, breathless.

Chloe nodded meekly. She had never thought of herself as a very
submissive person, but right now she felt like putty in his hands,
and she found herself liking it. "Let me know if it's too much, and I'll
stop." He said reassuringly, taking a deep breath, and adjusting his
bulging erection in his jeans.

"Okay," Chloe said, her heart beating faster as she ached to touch
his cock. He ran the finger of his free hand through her hair,
gripping firmly but gently at the crown of her head. Then he pulled
her head up to look at his face, and her body responded, a squeak
of pleasure escaping her lips. He grunted with pleasure as he
pushed his fingers back into her, now enthusiastically fucking her
with them. She couldn't hold her cries of pleasure in as her orgasm

built, holding on to the doorframe to stop herself from falling. She found the force of his grip electrifying, and her eyes closed, her pleasure beginning to peak. Her breathing changed to gasps as she readied herself, but she felt him slow his thrusting, and removing his fingers from inside of her again. "Not yet." He teased.

Still holding her hair firmly, he leant in for a deep and sensual kiss. She felt herself melting into it, and raised her hand to cup his face tenderly. His hand left her crotch, and stroked up her arm to her wrist, which he grabbed. Pulling away from the kiss, he looked her in the eyes, as if to read her expression. Her face was flushed, but her eyes glistened with excitement and anticipation. He let go of her hair and, stepping to the side, used her wrist to move her towards the kitchen island. She obliged with small steps, her jeans around her calves. He stepped behind her, slipping his hands under her shirt as he pushed her forward, her elbows and forearms resting on the counter. He pushed her top over her head, and she threw it to the floor as he continued to stroke her skin sensually. He was kissing her shoulders and back, gently working his way down her torso. Chloe shivered in anticipation, her breath becoming heavy. He reached her hips, and stroked the outside of her perky butt, before cupping her cheeks in a rough grip that made her gasp.

"Fuck," he whispered. Chloe wasn't sure if he had intended for her to hear or not, but a shiver of excitement ran through her. He must have noticed, because he grabbed another handful of her round behind and growled at her, "You like that?"

She nodded, struggling to put words together in that moment. She felt his grip change, and the rough material of his jeans met the soft skin of her naked backside. Ezra grunted, pushing himself against her, the bulge of his erect cock rubbing across her moistness. It felt good, and she moaned softly, pushing back against him. She had been so close to orgasm only a few minutes before, and had been denied. Her body was screaming for the release, and with his cock right there, every touch was beginning to feel like torture. Nonetheless, she was enjoying every second of being so intoxicatingly aroused. He was beginning to breathe heavily too, pushing his cock against her, and stopped with a grunt. Stepping back from her, she could hear his belt unbuckle, and she turned her head to see him step out of his pants, naked except for his shirt. His penis was rock hard, the tip glistening slightly, and he held it in his hand, stroking it slowly as he looked back at her.

"You have an amazing ass," he said, stepping back towards her. Her mind was foggy, with the sight of his cock exciting her more, she wanted him so badly. "Thanks," she managed in a whisper, her eyes locked on his thick shaft. He stepped up against her, the wetness of his tip touching her butt cheek and sending a bolt of excitement through her. With it so close to her entrance, she was overwhelmed with the urge to feel him inside of her. She gasped, and his other hand ran up her back, before pushing her chest down on the counter. Chloe moaned, her breasts crushed against the hard surface, almost crying from the intensity of her primal need for him. She could feel his hand brushing against her as he stroked himself, and his breath becoming heavy now, each breath audible, even from her position with her face almost against the bench. He was teasing her, and enjoying it, but Chloe could feel his own arousal getting the better of him. He grunted, and grabbed her ass firmly with his spare hand, before squatting down behind her.

Just the feeling of his breath on her wet slit was enough to cause Chloe to gasp. When his mouth met her clit she shivered, her body being flooded with waves of pleasure. He responded eagerly, his mouth working expertly, Chloe gasping and moaning softly as her pleasure built. Her breath caught in her mouth and she whimpered, her body shuddering uncontrollably with the intensity of the release it had been craving.

She could feel it, her juices flowing out of her as her vagina contracted. Ezra grunted from between her legs, drinking in her ejaculate excitedly. Chloe looked back at him, crouched behind her on the floor. It was an incredible sight, his hands gripping her thighs, his face suckling on her genitals, erect cock pulsing with excitement. "Oh fuck," she gasped, legs struggling to hold her weight post orgasm. Ezra moaned between her legs as she felt the impossible, she was cumming again. She gripped the counter for dear life as a second orgasm came, this one more intense than the last, a long and loud moan escaping her lips as her knees buckled, whole body shuddering. Ezra was practically holding her up, gasping for air as he pulled his face back, her juices dripping out of her. After a few deep breaths she looked back at him, still crouched on the floor, a small watery puddle beneath her, and wet droplets on his shirt. He looked from her quivering vagina to her face with a look of amazement. Ezra was stroking himself, seemingly unconsciously, "You alright?"

Chloe nodded weakly, struggling to catch her breath. Ezra stood up, his look of amazement turned to concern. "Do you need to lie down?"

Chloe didn't want to, and she paused for a second, focusing on her breath. She couldn't quite make herself form the words she wanted to; her brain felt like mashed potatoes. She bit her lip, and reluctantly nodded.

Ezra bent to help her out of her pants and boots. Her legs were shaking uncontrollably, and she was using the bench to steady herself. She was, however, slowly coming down from the high, and regaining control of her body. Gently, Ezra helped her stand, and she began to walk towards her bedroom, Ezra taking her hand to help her trembling legs. She allowed herself to collapse onto her bed ungracefully, the soft doona on her back helping her feel safe. She had never felt something of this intensity before, and although it felt wonderful, it was also a bit terrifying. Eyes closed, she lay there breathing deeply as she struggled to centre herself. Chloe felt Ezra's weight move on the mattress next to her. When she opened her eyes, he was lying next to her on his side, watching her, a look of concern on his face.

"Chloe," he said, seriously. "Are you okay?"

"Yeah," she said breathily, laughing a little at the situation. "Yeah, I am."

There was a small silence as she took a few more deep breaths, his eyes wandering over her body. He was concerned for her, but also obviously still aroused. "I've never felt that before," she managed. "Not like that. That was like my whole body just—"

He nodded as she stopped, forgetting what she was trying to say. She couldn't quite put her words together, and she felt a bit like she was floating, but she was still aching to feel him inside of her. She looked down towards his crotch, his penis still mostly hard. Ezra noticed her gaze, and his cock jumped with arousal. "It was incredibly hot," he said. "Watching you cum like that."

Chloe nodded, reaching for his cock. He inhaled as she began to stroke, the shaft returning quickly to full attention. "Chloe," he growled, body growing rigid with excitement.

She lifted her eyes to his, a moment of stillness between him, as she leaned in close. "Ezra," she whispered. "I want you to fuck me."

His eyes grew wide for a second as he processed what she had said, and then pushed himself forward, locking her in a passionate kiss. His penis pulsed in her hand, and she moaned in anticipation. He rolled her forward and reached back to unclasp her bra, her breasts falling slightly as they were released. Pulling back, he took in her naked body, running his hand over her curves as she lay there next to him. His fingers brushed over her exposed nipples, causing her to shiver slightly. "One sec," he said, getting up and heading back to the kitchen, where his jeans were.

Chloe rolled onto her back, stretching her arms up above her. She felt amazing. Not just physically, but mentally. The person she was only a few weeks ago seemed like a stranger to her. She was a new person, confident, powerful and sexy. Wanted and desirable, which was something she had always longed for, but now her happiness depended less on that. She was happy and carefree; she was loving it.

Ezra appeared back in the doorway, kneeling on the bed near her feet as he rolled the condom onto his rock-hard penis. He put his hands on her thighs, moving himself between them as he looked up at her face. He was biting his lip, and Chloe could not stop smiling.

This was it, the moment she had been longing for, fantasising about. She drew in a sharp breath as she felt the head of his penis brush against the outside of her. Ezra reached down, stroking the length of her wetness with the tip. He inhaled sharply too, finding her opening and sliding the tip in. Placing both his hands on either side of her waist, he slowly guided the rest of himself into her. Chloe felt herself stretching slightly, his girth more than any she had felt before, and she gasped involuntarily. It was a wonderful feeling, and she melted into it with a soft moan. With a grunt, Ezra began his thrusting, slowly at first, but soon increasing in speed. She was moaning softly, almost a whimper, as she lay helpless beneath him, her pleasure building rapidly. His breathing was laboured, and sweat was forming on his body. Suddenly she felt herself peaking, and grabbed his arm with her hand. Gasping for air and closing her eyes, she orgasmed, throwing her head back into the pillow as her body shuddered. Ezra stopped moving, gritting his teeth, and moaning as he felt her muscles contract around him. Chloe calmed, relaxing into the softness of the bed as her orgasm subsided. "Holy fuck," he whispered. "That feels amazing."

Ezra resumed his thrusts, grunting deeply now, only managing a few before his rhythm started to falter. "Will you tell me when you're going to cum again?" She nodded, unable to speak through her post-orgasmic haze. He straightened up, grabbing her hips with his broad hands as he pulled her roughly against him with a satisfied grunt. Chloe moaned softly as she watched him above her, eyes wide, his grunts getting more unrestrained. He slammed her body against his, making an audible wet, fleshy tap each time, and she once again felt the familiar swell of arousal. The force of his thrusts was making her breasts bounce, and she grabbed them with her hands, squeezing them gently as she readied herself to cum again. She let out a soft cry and he met her gaze. This was it.

"I'm…" she gasped out desperately, but he understood. His fingers gripped her, almost hurting, and she began to shudder, a long, unrestrained moan escaping from her. This orgasm was more intense than the last. Ezra must have felt it too, because he thrust a few times, slowly and deeply, a cry of release escaping his mouth. Chloe gasped for breath, releasing her grip on her own breasts, noticing she had left marks with her fingernails. Ezra backed away from her, sweating and panting, and then let himself collapse onto the bed next to her. Chloe panted a few times before she was able to control her breath, and turn to face Ezra. He was lying on his back, hands on his head, his face an expression of absolute elation. He was grinning from ear to ear, laughing quietly to himself. "Holy fuck, Chloe," he said, shaking his head in disbelief. "How the fuck did I get so lucky?"

She lay her head down, smiling to herself. "I could ask myself the same thing."

Chapter 11

Chloe was happy she had splurged on the extra avocado today, as she munched her way through a salad wrap on her lunch break. It wasn't very often she allowed herself these little extras, being frugal by nature, but her life was going great recently. Somehow, feeling good about herself meant she was more confident with ordering extra avocado in her wrap. It had been three months since Ezra and she had first slept together, and they had built a strong friendship. They seemed to both recognise that their relationship was physical and fun, nothing serious. Which was just what she needed right now. After all, she was physically attracted to Ezra, but imagining a long future with him? It just didn't feel right. It wasn't that she couldn't see herself in a polyamorous relationship. No, in fact she was feeling like it was a much better fit for her than monogamy ever was. It was just that Ezra didn't seem like serious relationship material, at least not for Chloe. After all, they never really talked about anything. Sure, they had conversations, but it was mostly about pop culture, the people they knew, or just silly jokes. She didn't really know the first thing about him, and he didn't really know her at all. He only knew her body. Chloe smirked to herself at the thought. She used to have such a strong connection between sex and love, but she was happy how things were going now. She felt independent, confident, attractive and sexually satisfied.

The sound of the chair opposite her moving startled her, and Ezra sat casually, his woody cologne making Chloe grin. She nodded a greeting at him, her mouth full of delicious avocado and salad. He started attacking some kind of Asian noodle dish, small drops of soy sauce splashing onto the table. A slight tingle of annoyance ran through Chloe, but she pushed it aside. She had been noticing little things like that about Ezra lately – how he would make a mess and never clean up when he left, how he would happily let laundry and dishes pile up at home until Avery got around to doing them. They niggled at the back of her mind, urging her to say something. Instead she shook her head, trying to physically push the thoughts away. She couldn't really let those things bother her too much, after all, he wasn't really her boyfriend or anything. They weren't serious.

As amazing as she was feeling these days, there was a lot on her mind she just couldn't shake. I was a year this week since Sam and her had broken up, and as much as she had thought she'd moved on, the pain from that betrayal had resurfaced once she realised the date that morning. She had no plans for the weekend, having reached out to the girls and found them all busy, and was dreading spending it alone. She had come so far as a person that the last thing she wanted was end up drunkenly Facebook stalking her ex. Not healthy.

Chloe tucked her loose hair behind her ear as she eyed his food, "How's the noodles?"
Ezra nodded enthusiastically, swallowing his mouthful before answering. "Good. And your burrito?"

"Fine," she replied, her voice flatter than she intended it to be. She noticed his head tilt slightly, as if he could tell from her tone something was wrong. She quickly took another bite of her burrito to avoid talking.

He leaned forward, his face softening. "Chloe, are you okay?"

"Yeah," she said dismissively, finishing her mouthful. Maybe he had time to see her on the weekend. A physical distraction would be as good as any. "Are you free at all on the weekend?"

Ezra glanced around, seemingly casual, but making sure nobody was nearby before he spoke. "I got a family thing Sunday and a date Saturday night, but I'm free in the afternoon."
A pang of jealousy hit Chloe as she heard the word "date". *A date? And not with me?* She cringed at her own thoughts. *Ezra can go on dates with other people, Chloe.* She told herself sternly. Outwardly, she nodded, smiling slightly. "Is it okay if I come over for a bit on Saturday?"

"Of, course," he said. He paused, studying her face for a moment. "You know if anything is bothering you, you can talk to me, right?" He leaned forward, lowering his voice. "After all I am you boyfr—"

He was cut off by Carla, who plopped down on an empty chair, her plate making a loud noise as it connected with the table in front of her "Sorry!" she exclaimed, face beaming.
Ezra leaned back quickly, as if he realised he was still in the work lunchroom. Chloe was trying her best to keep her face neutral, looking down at her plate. *He was going to say he was my boyfriend?* Chloe's mind was buzzing with a sudden panic. *But he's Avery's boyfriend really. We're just.... I don't know. Having fun... Aren't we?* Carla took a bite of her sandwich and leaned back in her chair casually. "Any plans for the weekend, Ez?"

Ezra shrugged nonchalantly, completely ignoring the nickname she had just given him, "Not really."
His eyes moved to Chloe, smiling cheekily. "What about you,

Chlo?"

"Ah," she started, her voice shaking slightly. Her brain was buzzing, making it hard to put up a happy front. She desperately wanted to hold it together, but she couldn't help the heavy sadness in her stomach. "Nothing. I've got no plans."

Carla narrowed her eyes, seeing plain as day that Chloe was upset. Carla looked down at her phone, which was on the table and, seeing the date, inhaled sharply. Her head whipped back to Chloe as a wave of realisation rushed over her. "Oh Chloe! It's this week isn't it?"

Chloe broke. Hearing it out loud was like taking a hammer to her already cracking wall of emotion. She nodded, lowering her head to hide the tears brimming in her eyes, despite her best efforts to stop them. *Fuck Chloe,* she scolded herself. *This is just embarrassing. It was a year ago. You should be over this by now. Stop being pathetic.*

"It's old news," she whispered.

Ezra was looking from Carla to Chloe, his face a map of puzzlement. He was desperately trying to understand what was wrong, but he had no idea. Carla leaned forward and placed a hand on Chloe's, comforting her slightly. She turned to Ezra, "It's been a year since she broke up with Sam."

Understanding washed over Ezra's face as Chloe nodded meekly, feeling very uncomfortable showing so much emotion in the middle of the lunch room. She had told Ezra the basics, but their relationship was physical and fun, she didn't want to muddy it up with such intense emotions, and details about her past. It was too painful. In fact, the only person she had told everything to was Carla, because she was there at the time, and her therapist. Talking about it made it real, and Chloe was doing her best to convince herself that it had never happened. Or at least, that it had happened to someone else.

Calm down, she told herself sternly. Taking a few deep breaths, she wiped her face, pushing the tears away. Feeling a bit ridiculous, she laughed a little, "Oh fuck, I'm sorry."

"Don't be sorry," Carla said gently, squeezing her hand. "It was a big thing for you. Heck, a breakup like that would be a big thing for anyone."

Chloe nodded, eyes down at her hands, which were now in her lap. "I guess so." she said. *Doesn't stop me from feeling like an absolute asshole for still being so cut up about it,* she thought.

"You were together seven years," Carla continued, as Chloe focused on her breathing. "You trusted him, and he betrayed that trust. It's natural for you to feel like this." Chloe nodded, and Carla continued, leaning in to her. "And then, on top of cheating on you he blamed you for it. I mean it's ridiculous. Classic gas-lighting. I know I told you then but I want you to remember how proud I am of you, for going over there and confronting him. Even though-" Chloe flashed her eyes up to Carla's, screaming silently *STOP.* She was only making it worse. Carla's words seemed to catch in her mouth as she registered Chloe's expression. "Uh... yeah. Anyway, I'm proud of you. Of how well you are doing without him. I mean look at you!"

Chloe was painfully aware of Ezra's eyes on her. She knew how she must look right now, puffy eyed and emotional, and she silently wished she was anywhere else right now. The idea of it was bizarre, he had seen her naked countless times, from every angle, but it was now that she felt the most vulnerable in front of him. Something must have registered with him too because he was dead silent, looking anywhere but at Chloe's face. *Oh no,* she thought, a sudden catastrophic thought hitting her like a tonne of bricks. *He thinks I'm an absolute loser for still being so caught up about my ex. He won't want to be with me if he thinks I'm such a stage five clinger. Fuck Chloe, you've fucked it up again.* Chloe felt the anxiety rise in her chest. Suddenly she room felt much too crowded. The trio were silent, Carla's last sentence hanging heavily in the air. What do you even say after that? Ezra was poking at his noodles, glancing up at Chloe and she finished her burrito as quickly as she could, despite the tense knot in her stomach. She stood up and walked away briskly, mouth still full of food. She needed to be anywhere but here right now.

Focusing on her breath, Chloe strode confidently out of the lunchroom and into the hallway that led to the staffroom. Chloe was forcing her brain to focus on work, listing to herself what she needed to get done that afternoon. Stopping for a moment to catch her breath, she heard the door from the lunchroom swing open behind her, making her jump. It was Ezra, who stood for a moment, silently, before heading to a door opposite where she was standing. It was the stairwell that led down to the shop floor and basement levels, and up to the roof. He paused for a moment, eying her with genuine concern. He gestured with his head for her to enter the stairwell with him, and she hesitated, looking towards the staffroom. "I have to get back to work." she said meekly. *He's going to break it off with you.* Her mind spun. She wanted to avoid that conversation more than anything.

"I just want a minute," Ezra said softly, taking her hand. Suddenly, her anxiety melted away. *He seems genuinely concerned*, she thought with surprise.

Chloe hesitated, then stepped into the stairwell, making sure nobody saw her going in. Ezra closed the door gently behind her, shutting them off from the rest of the world.

The stairwell was cold, being thick brick walls designed to stop a fire. Completely windowless, it was lit only by a few florescent lights, which were old, and gave off a yellow light. It smelt like damp concrete in there. Chloe hugged herself involuntarily.

Ezra stepped towards Chloe and wrapped her tight in a bear hug. Her breath caught in her chest and she squeaked a little in surprise.

"I'm so sorry Chloe," he said, one of his hands cupping her head. "You deserve better than that."

"I know," she said, pushing her head back so she could speak. "I don't like talking about it much though."

He looked down at her, his eyes searching her face. "What do you mean?"

She shrugged as much as she could in the tight embrace. *I mean I don't want to talk about it.* She thought with annoyance. "I just want to move on."

His face melted into an expression of kindness, "You can talk to me." His hand moved to her cheek, cupping her face gently. "You can trust me, Chloe. What he did to you is wrong, but it is real. And you need to talk about things to heal."

Chloe looked down. She wasn't sure what to say exactly. Ezra was right, her therapist had said as much too, and she knew it was true. She had convinced herself that if she didn't talk about it, and pretended it never happened, maybe she would just forget it. But she couldn't help feeling pissed off at Ezra. She had just said she didn't want to talk about it, and he was pushing the issue.

 She looked up at him, ready to tell him again that she didn't want to talk and to just drop it, but his face was so gentle. She ran one of her hands through his beard, the thick hair soft against her fingers. *Maybe I can trust him,* she thought. She took a deep breath and sighed.

"Sam went to a party without me," she started. "Which wasn't unusual. He liked to go out all night and party. I wasn't really into that... scene." She stalled. "He'd started taking drugs. Just recreationally, but I wasn't into that. You know, that's not my thing. So, I didn't go. We had a fight a few months before I found out, he wanted me to do drugs with him. I said no. He told me my mind would never be truly open until I had experienced it, but..." she shook her head, scoffing at the memory.

"My confidence was so small," she continued, looking down at her feet. "You know, it was years in that relationship and he made me feel like I couldn't be anything without him. I decided on my degree to suit his, took jobs which he approved of. Even wore my hair the way he liked." She stepped back, leaning against the railing on the landing. She was avoiding looking at Ezra.

"I'm sorry, I sound pathetic." The words just tumbled out, and she flashed her eyes up to him as she said them in panic. "I just- I don't want you to think less of me, I guess."

The air in the stairwell was thick and dank. Ezra was standing there, silent. He was listening to her every word. "Chlo, I would never." his baritone voice was kind, easing away her anxiety.

For the first time in a long time, she felt safe to talk about the most traumatic experience of her life. "A friend had come back from over east for the week, and went to this party with Sam. He texted me, told me everything." She took a deep breath. It was tough, but she could do this. "He had been seeing someone else for ten months. I was furious. I wasn't thinking straight, and I just jumped in my car."

Blinking the tears from her eyes, she gripped the wheel of her car so hard her knuckles were turning white. Her breath was ragged, coming in between her teeth. She was barely holding herself back from screaming and crying. Furious, shocked and sad all at once, it was like she was possessed. She didn't even know exactly where the party was, but she knew the suburb. She was just driving, hell bent on confronting Sam. She sure as hell wasn't thinking straight. Jason's message played through her head, taunting her.

He's cheating on you, has been for 10 months.

All the guys know and just nobody wanted to be the one to tell you

It was like a knife in her gut, twisting every time she thought of another person who knew, and had been watching her make a fool out of herself for months. Like some sort of idiot, she had trusted

him.

She turned onto the main road of the suburb, rolling her window down to see if she could hear any music. Nothing. Randomly she turned right into a side street, and began making guesses at how to weave through the suburb. Nothing. Just dark houses of families sleeping peacefully. She was the only car on the road, which was lucky. She wasn't exactly driving well right now.

It felt like a long time before she heard a faint bass beat. The house was maybe two or three streets away. It was almost like the fire in her belly had been stoked, and she drove back and forth through the winding streets, cursing as she hit a dead end, and had to go back. Eventually, she saw the house, cars parked abstractly on the lawn, and stopped on the side of the road a few houses down. From her car, she could hear the beat of the electronic music, and the occasional shout and cheer of people. It sounded like a wonderful and lively party. Now that she was here, all of her enthusiasm seemed to drain from her. What exactly was she planning to do, anyway? Storm in there in her oversized shirt and sweatpants, eyes red from crying, demand to see Sam, and what? Everyone at that party knew she was being cheated on. She was the butt of this joke. Hell, she wasn't even wearing shoes. She'd just be embarrassing herself further.

And what if that isn't even the right party? Defeated, Chloe sat in her car, staring at the house, tears silently falling from her eyes. It was over, all those years and it was just... over. After some time, she slowly turned the key and began driving home.

The exit to Sam's house was before hers and impulsively, she took it instead. She couldn't bear to go home right now, it's not like she could sleep, and she just felt like it was the only thing she could do.

She felt powerless as she pulled up on a side street opposite his house, noticing his car wasn't in the driveway. She wasn't sure why, but she felt like she didn't want his family to see her out there on the street, in her car, in the middle of the night. Where she had parked was far enough away that they wouldn't notice it was her, but she could still clearly see the house. Did they know, too? Had he bought this other girl back here to his house, introduced her to his parents too? She felt sick.

She sat in her car for half an hour. Then it became an hour, two, three. Chloe felt hopeless, she didn't want to leave without confronting Sam about this cheating. The night stretched on, and Chloe entered a state of resignation. This was it— the end of her life as she knew it. They wouldn't buy the place together they had been planning for months. Wouldn't get engaged or married. No kids, no regular holidays. All those plans they had made. All empty promises. All lies.

The more she thought about it, the more she realised all feelings she had had for him had evaporated. Her heart was painfully empty, the thought of him kissing her, touching her, having sex with her, all made her feel sick. The thought suddenly struck Chloe that he might have been having sex with this girl, and then coming home and having sex with her in the same day. She tasted bile as her stomach churned at the idea.

Suddenly his car rolled into the driveway, and Sam's lanky figure lumbered out of the car, heading for the front door. Checking the time now, it was early in the morning. Chloe hadn't slept a wink, but it looked like Sam was the one worse for wear. A wave of terror overcame her as she hesitated, the conflict now imminent. . It might have been the lack of sleep or pure fury, but Chloe launched herself out of her car, tucking her phone in her pocket of her sweatpants, bare feet stinging as she marched across the cold bitumen. She opened her mouth to yell at him, but her throat was so dry and ragged, a strained "Uh" was all that came out. By the time she reached the corner opposite the house, Sam had managed to open the front door and step inside, completely oblivious to her. Chloe charged across the street, feet pounding, but Sam didn't notice, and shut the door behind him.

Chloe wanted to scream, now standing right in front of Sam's house. She couldn't very well knock on the door at this hour, and the garage was closed. Having dated Sam as long as she had, she knew his parents often left the back door unlocked so they could easily let the cat out. The grass was cold and wet under her bare feet as she crossed it, coming to the gate on the side of the house, rising on her tiptoes to undo the latch. It swung open and she shut it behind her, the latch making a loud click which echoed sharply through the silence of the night. Chloe flinched as the sound echoed through the quiet suburb, but kept going towards the back of the house. The limestone pavers she was now creeping across felt ice cold under her bare feet, the fence and double story house looming above her, making a narrow and dark passage towards the backyard. She rounded the corner, and saw the back door was slightly open. Without thinking, she headed straight for it, slipping into the house as silently as she could, and making her way towards the stairs that lead up to the second storey, where Sam's bedroom was. She was breathing heavily now, both from fear and rage, and before she knew it, she was in front of his bedroom door. She was acutely aware of how insane she was being right now, but it was if she was outside of herself. The light was on in his room, and she could hear him shuffling about. She had come too far now to second-guess herself, and she entered without saying a word.

Sam was standing near his desk, his shirt dumped on the floor next to the washing basket, a shocked look on his face. His eyes were wide as he took her in, bloodshot and dilated. For the first time she saw him not as the man she loved, but as a stranger, and it struck her just how unattractive he had become. No longer the fit and charismatic boy she had fallen in love with years ago. Now he was pale and thin, deep bags formed under his eyes from many nights of poor sleep. His jeans, which she had helped him pick out a year ago, were noticeably baggy on his frame, held up by a belt which had additional holes roughly punched in it. His short beard, which was usually nicely trimmed for work, was uncombed, giving him a wild look.

"What the fuck Chloe?" he hissed, his shock quickly changing to anger. His eyes darted to the door which led from his room to the bathroom, and back to her. He licked his lips nervously, the fingers of his left hand twitching. Chloe's stomach flipped; she had never seen him acting like this before. She stepped into his room, closing the door behind her.

"You've been cheating on me," she spat, barely able to contain her rage. His expression dropped from his face for a second, before he curled his lip back, as if in disbelief. "No," he said, shaking his head.

Furious, Chloe pulled her phone from her pocket, and charged across the room towards him. She thrust the screen in his face to show the texts from Jason. "What the fuck is this then?"
He looked at the screen for all of a second before pushing her arm away with his forearm and scoffing dismissively. His eyes darted around the room as Chloe seethed. This close to him, he smelt awful, like warm beer, old sweat and smoke. He looked at her face, and Chloe shivered at the emptiness in his expression. It was if he

couldn't really see her there at all. He shrugged, the gesture making his lanky arms bounce at his sides. "So?"

"What, you aren't going to deny it?" Chloe was baffled. She had expected something, a confession, an apology, denial. She felt like her heart was shattering in her chest and he seemed to not care at all.

He smirked, moving to walk past her, toward the bathroom door. Chloe was exhausted, heartbroken, shocked and furious. Without thinking, she grabbed his arm, "The fuck is wrong with you, Sam?"

He pulled his arm away from her with such force that it turned her whole body. "Crazy bitch," he muttered, moving towards the bathroom again. Chloe stepped towards him. She was not about to let him leave without having some sort of resolution.

Sam flinched at her moving towards him, and turned to look at her with an expression of disgust. His eyes were glassy and teeth bared, his breath smelt horribly metallic. Before Chloe could react, his hand was on her shoulder, pushing her away. He might have been thin, but he pushed her with such unexpected force that she fell backwards, her back connecting with the edge of his wardrobe with a distinct thud. Luckily, Chloe managed to catch herself before she fell completely. Sam stood still for a moment, silently looking at her. His expression was unreadable, but to Chloe, he looked frighteningly detached. He turned and walked into the bathroom, quietly shutting the door behind him. The soft click of the lock punctuated the silence.

Pain and panic swept over Chloe. Her back radiated heat from next to her shoulder blade, her arm tingling slightly from the impact. She was in shock, frozen in place for what felt like an eternity, tears brimming in her eyes. She heard the shower start in the bathroom, which caught her breath in her chest. Adrenaline filled her body, and she began to move, practically holding her breath as she flew down the stairs and out the front door, not caring how loud it was as she shut it. She ran as fast as she could into the cold and silent night, back to her car, back to safety.

Silence hung in the air, heavy with the cool dampness of the concrete walls. Chloe had been looking at the ground in front of Ezra's feet as she had revealed, in complete detail, the horrific night her world had fallen apart. Retelling it, she could feel all the emotions she had felt that night. When she had spoken about Sam shoving her into the wardrobe, she had paused, unsure whether to tell that detail to Ezra, but pushed through, her stomach in knots as she explained it in detail. Ezra had grunted disapprovingly when she had revealed that detail to him, but stayed frowning, arms folded. Chloe looked up and him, tears brimming in her eyes. She felt small and vulnerable, having laid all her baggage out in front of him, and was now waiting for him to reject her.

She studied his face as he looked at the ground, probably trying to process everything. It was a lot, Chloe knew, especially for someone with their kind of relationship. Then his eyes met hers, and they were tender, caring and understanding. He unfolded his arms and reached out to her, and she broke, falling into his arms, her face buried in his chest as she cried deeply. The warmth of his embrace, and his cologne comforted her as she gripped his broad back with her small fingers. He kissed the top of her head tenderly, her fear melting away, replaced with a feeling of calm. She was safe now, here with Ezra.

Burying her face in his chest, her tears stopped and she snuggled in, wishing to disappear into him. His hand was absentmindedly stroking her back as she lifted her face to look at him. He was staring blankly ahead, but looked down with a soft smile when he noticed her looking.

She pulled back, wiping her face. They were still at work, an environment where they usually kept up appearances of just friendship. Reality washed over Chloe, and her blood ran cold. Had she crossed a line without even realising it?

Ezra was still silent, his eyes sad as he looked at her. The air was heavy with the silence.
"Chlo," his baritone voice echoed in the concrete space as he dropped his shoulders. "I don't know what to say."

Chloe shrugged, laughing awkwardly. "Yeah, it's one of those things, I guess," she looked at him with a half-smile, forcing herself to sound nonchalant. "There's nothing really to say."
Ezra nodded, and Chloe shuffled her feet on the concrete landing, watching the dust and dirt shift under her booted toe.

"You deserve better," Ezra whispered.

Chloe nodded. "I do." The silence fell again. It made her feel uncomfortable. Shrugging, Chloe stepped towards the door. "I really do need to get back to work."

Chloe reached for the door handle, but as she gripped it, Ezra placed his hand on hers. She looked up at him, his face so close to hers she could feel his breath on her neck. "I care about you, Chloe. A lot."

She smiled meekly. "I care about you a lot too."

He bent down, his free hand cupping the back of her head as he pulled her into a deep kiss. Chloe's heart filled with warmth as she felt, for the first time with Ezra, real romance.
He let her go and she stood there for a moment, still, studying his face to see if he had felt it too. He smiled, eyes glinting. Chloe was sure he had.

Ezra laughed a little, lifting his hand from hers. "Yeah, we should get back to work."

Chapter 12

Chloe rapped her knuckles on the hard wood door of Ezra and Avery's house, tapping out a playful pattern with her knock. She had spent the entirety of Saturday morning busying herself by getting ready to go to Ezra's house that afternoon, succeeding in distracting herself from any creeping negative feelings associated with this week. As a result, she found herself in an excellent mood as she strode up the path towards their front door, the previously overgrown flowers trimmed back slightly, but as fragrant and inviting as ever. She could hear cicadas in the garden, welcoming her to the house, as the afternoon sun warmed her back. She had chosen to dress simply today, in her favourite jeans and an oversized shirt.

The heavy door swung open, and she was greeted by Avery's beaming smile. Her hair was loose around her shoulders, and she was wearing a large, pale blue men's dress shirt. She had used a belt to accentuate her waist, and her long tan legs reached out from below the hem. Chloe was not expecting Avery to answer the door, and she was definitely not expecting her to be only wearing a shirt. Without thinking, she blurted out "you look amazing, Avery."

"Thanks," she beamed, a bounce in her step as she stepped back to allow Chloe to enter the living space. Ezra exited the kitchen as Chloe passed Avery, putting a glass of wine in her hand with a smile. "How are you doing?"

Chloe accepted the wine, taking a quick sniff of the glass to gauge the sweetness of it before taking a sip. "Good, actually," she returned his smile. "I'm being adequately distracted."

Avery brushed past Chloe as she headed to the couch, and Chloe noticed the light, sweet perfume that she wore, making her smell like candy. It was almost the opposite of Ezra's earthy scent, which still made her stomach flip whenever she smelled it. She followed Avery, noticing with a laugh that the coffee table was completely covered in beauty items, leaving nowhere for her to place her glass.

"Sorry!" Avery said, scooping an armful of facemasks into a small plastic basket. "I got them all out to see which ones you might want to do, but I just made a mess."

"Facemasks?" Chloe said, curiously. "I've never done a facemask before."

Avery's eyes widened in amazement. "No way! Well, you'll love it, I promise."

She grabbed a colourful bag, opening it to show Chloe a vast collection of nail polish bottles "I thought we could do a whole beauty day, once Ezra leaves of course, just us two girls." She winked. "A metamour date."

Chloe had read that word before, metamour. The person who was also dating your partner, but who you yourself were not dating. It was the first time it had occurred to her that that's what she and Avery were. As much as she had gotten along with Avery, she just couldn't shake the feeling that there needed to be some separation between them, or their whole relationship would fall apart. She couldn't quite put her finger on exactly why she got this feeling, but she was sure it was the case. Starting to spend time with just her felt like a big deal.

Ezra sat down next to Chloe, and seeing her stunned facial expression, took her hand. "You okay babe?"

Chloe blinked, and nodded. *That's the first time he called me Babe,* she thought with slight surprise. "Yeah, I think so." She pursed her lips and looked at Avery. "Are you really okay with being my friend? I mean…" Chloe closed her eyes, trying to make sense of what she was trying to say. "I mean, I'm kind of seeing Ezra. Are you sure you want to be my friend too? It seems kind of like a big deal."

Avery tiled her head, eyes squinting as she thought. She shook her head. "You know, I hadn't even thought about it that way. I think you're cool Chloe, and I want to be your friend. The fact that you're dating my boyfriend doesn't even come into that, it's a separate thing." She smiled, placing her hand on Chloe's knee. "I am glad he's seeing you though."

Ezra laughed, "Why, so you can both talk about me behind my back?"

Avery stuck out her tongue playfully, and Ezra leaned forward to grab her and pull her into a playful kiss. Chloe couldn't help but laugh at the whole situation. When she was around those two, together, all the tension and stress seemed to leave her body. They had such a fun and relaxed energy that all pretence just slipped away. Chloe had never felt more comfortable around anyone else before. Perhaps she was silly for thinking spending time with Avery would be an issue. It's just two new friends doing facemasks and nails, how could that possibly make anything more complicated?

"I guess I just think what we have is kind of great." Chloe said, shrugging, as the couple turned to look at her. "I've been through a lot, and I know other people have been through worse but, you know, I haven't ever had many people really want me around. I've felt like I've just been space-filling for other people for years and I don't feel like that at all with you guys. I feel like you genuinely want me here. The fact that you have gone out of your way to do this for me, to even make time for me, to try and help me through a tough time means a lot to me. You are both really special to me. What we have is really special to me. And I just... I don't want to ruin it."

Ezra looked at her, his eyes noticeably wet as he smiled. "Chloe—"

He was cut off by Avery leaping onto her, enveloping her in an enthusiastic hug. "You can't ruin it, my friend! If anything, it will only make it better."

Chloe laughed, but watched Ezra as he turned away from them, and headed into the kitchen. Avery's soft hair had fallen into her face as they hugged, and as Ezra left, Chloe pushed it aside, her fingers stroking Avery's shoulder. The floral scent of her shampoo struck her nose, and Chloe was suddenly very aware of just how close their bodies were to each other. The thought sent a tingle through her chest.

Stunned at her own reaction, Chloe pulled back from the hug and grabbed at her drink, taking two generous sips. But before she could open her mouth to speak, Ezra re-entered the room, whiskey in hand. "Should we watch a movie?"

Avery searched through Netflix, and put on an early 2000s horror film, enthusing about how good it was to Chloe. "You'll love it, I'm sure of it."

It wasn't long into the movie that Chloe started exchanging looks with Ezra, the wooden acting on the screen anything but good. The lead actress turned to face the camera, a lacklustre scream escaping her mouth.

Avery burst into a fit of laughter, "Oh my god this film is horrible!"

Chloe nodded, "I thought you said it was good?"

Avery shook her head, tears of laughter forming in her eyes. "I remembered it differently I guess."

Ezra's phone buzzed from the table. His eyes widened, and he looked at the two women. "Mel wants to meet earlier." He looked from Avery to Chloe, as if waiting for them to grant him permission to go.

Avery stared back at him, eyebrows raised. "And Chloe only just got here."

He looked at Chloe, who felt a twang of guilt for being there. She was only invited so she wouldn't be lonely, and Ezra already had these plans, after all. "No, it's okay. Go."

Ezra practically leapt out of his seat and flew out of the room, Chloe's heart sinking at his eagerness. Despite what she had said, she really had been looking forward to spending time with Ezra. Watching him so excited to leave felt a little bit like a rejection. *Stop it Chloe, you're reading too much into this,* she told herself sternly. Chloe noticed Avery studying her face with a concerned expression, and Chloe forced a smile.

Avery raised her eyebrows at Chloe, obviously seeing right through her. But she didn't say anything, and simply turned back to the movie, sipping her drink.

Chloe and Avery sat in silence for about ten minutes, but for Chloe it felt like an eternity. Watching the main actress trying to avoid the killer, fumbling from room to room, making stupid decisions. She wanted to tell Ezra to stay, but she didn't speak. She couldn't speak. She desperately didn't want to be the crazy jealous girlfriend that Ezra now knew she could be. *Keep your cool, Chloe.* She told herself, pushing her bubbling feelings down.

A flurry of movement behind them as Ezra swept into the room, now wearing a neatly pressed dress shirt and filling his pockets with his belongings. He swirled his keys around his finger as he picked them up, a bounce in his step. He leaned over the couch, plating a kiss on Avery's cheek, and one on the top of Chloe's head.

"Ezra," Avery said, a hint of annoyance in her voice. "Kiss her properly."

Ezra broke out in a grin as he leaned down, hand cupping the back of Chloe's head, and passionately kissed her. Chloe felt her annoyance at him melt away as the smell of his cologne filled her nostrils, the slight taste of straight whiskey on his breath.

"Have fun, ladies!" he shouted behind himself as he shut the heavy front door, his enthusiasm carrying him out into the world.

Avery rolled her eyes, and slumped in her chair. "I can't believe he just ditched you like that."

Chloe blinked, surprised at Avery's reaction. "Yeah, I'm a little annoyed about it."

"A little?" Avery scoffed, tossing back the last of her drink. "You had it written all over your face, girl. You're pissed."

Chloe looked down at her feet, embarrassed. Yeah, she was pissed. But she didn't realise she was doing such a bad job of keeping it to herself.

"I mean, yeah." Chloe admitted. "I kind of thought I'd get to spend a little time with him."
She looked at Avery and shrugged, "I was kind of an add-on plan though. He had that date with Mel organised before me."

"So?" Avery said, standing up. "He was *dating* you before her. You're his freaking girlfriend, he can't treat you like that." She looked at her empty glass with annoyance. "Ugh, I need another drink."

She stormed into the kitchen, and Chloe, who was close to finishing her drink too, grabbed her glass and followed. "Avery?"

Avery put the bottle down on the bench with a heavy sigh. She tucked her hair behind her ear, and Chloe could see she was clearly upset. "Are you okay?"

Avery shook her head, her mouth pressed tightly together. She looked at Chloe and her eyes were wet; she was holding back tears. "Every time he does something like this," she gestured towards the front door emphatically, "I just feel a huge pang of fear."

She took a sip of her drink, and turned so her back rested on the bench. Staring into her glass sadly, she whispered, "What if he finds someone better and doesn't want to be with me anymore?"

"Avery!" Chloe stepped forward and wrapped her metamour in a warm hug, placing her glass on the bench as she did so. Avery leaned into her, her dark hair falling against Chloe's chest as she placed her head on her shoulder. Avery didn't cry, but she sighed deeply, and Chloe felt the tension and stress melt away from her soft body as they embraced. The air felt still around the pair, and Chloe felt a warmth rising in her chest. The fruity smell of her hair, the softness of her skin. Chloe suddenly became very aware of Avery's chest pressing against her own as she breathed. Her stomach flipped, and impulsively she stepped back.
Avery wiped her eyes, and laughed, tossing her head to rearrange

her hair out of her face. "Do you want to watch something a bit better, maybe?"

Chloe laughed, "Definitely. This movie is horrible."

Avery nodded, heading back to the couch, "I know! I can't believe I ever thought it was good."

Chloe winced as she sipped her wine through a straw, the wet sheet mask making it impossible to do it any other way. Avery laughed at her, rolling back into the couch cushions as she did so. She was tipsy now, her movements becoming loose and clumsy. Chloe knew she would need to go home soon, so had been pacing herself more with her drinks.

Nonetheless, she was finding herself becoming more relaxed and open in Avery's company.
"Which colour do you think?" Avery grabbed at the nail polish while still laying down on the couch, holding up two bottles. "Pink or purple?"

Chloe shrugged, "Why not both?"

Avery's eyes widened. "Oh my God. Yes!"

Chloe put her glass down on the table, and shuffled through the polish colours herself. There was a moment of silence as Avery began painting, and it suddenly occurred to Chloe that she didn't know much about how Avery and Ezra met. Before she could stop herself, she blurted out, "So how long have you and Ezra been together?"

Avery didn't break concentration on her nails. "Six years now." She said. She looked up at Chloe as she placed the brush back into the pot. "We met online, through a game. I lived in over east but was really looking to get away from my parents." She turned back to her nails, "but that's another story. Anyway, I got on a plane and here I am."

Chloe couldn't contain the surprise on her face. "That's a lot to risk on a guy you've never met."

Avery shrugged, "I know. I kind of figured that, even if it didn't work out, I was at least far away from my parents." She broke into a grin. "Working out well so far, though."

"Yeah," Chloe agreed, unscrewing the top of the nail polish colour she had chosen, a dark burgundy. "If I can ask, what was so bad about your parents?"

Avery laughed, but her voice was tinged with sadness. "They are religious. Very religious." She dunked the brush in the pot, collecting more colour, and continued without looking up at Chloe. "They wanted me to not only save myself for marriage, but find a nice boy from church. Needless to say, I'm a bit of a family disappointment."

Chloe chucked, "You're far from a disappointment in my eyes."

Avery looked up at her, and smiled. "Thank you. That's a really nice thing to say."

"No problem," Chloe shrugged. "It's pretty easy to just tell the truth."
There was a moment of silence, as the two women studiously pained their nails, until Avery spoke. "In the interest of being truthful," she said "Can I ask you a question?"

"Sure," Chloe responded without hesitation.

"How many people have you slept with?"

Chloe dunked her brush calmly as her heartbeat pounded in her ears. "Define slept with."

Avery's eyes widened as a smirk crossed her face, "Just sex, you know. What the kids would call a home run."

Chloe mimed thinking, which made Avery laugh. "Three. Including Ezra."

Avery nodded. "So, Ezra, your dickhead ex-boyfriend and…" She paused for dramatic effect. "Another high school boyfriend?"

Chloe blushed. "Not exactly."

"Oh!" Avery sat upright, waving her nails to dry them. Her eyes were glistening cheekily. "A summer fling? One-night stand? Tell me everything!"

Chloe smiled to herself, shaking her head. "No, nothing like that. We were sort of dating, only for a few weeks, but we had to keep it a secret. It was high school." Seeing Avery's confusion, she sighed. "Her name was Jessica."

There was a long pause where Chloe could feel her heart pounding in her chest. She hadn't revealed that to anyone in a long time. In fact, the last person she had told was Sam. He had either completely forgot about it through the course of their relationship, or not taken her seriously, because he had made unintentionally hurtful comments about queer people late in their relationship. Now that she thought about it, though, she wasn't so sure they were unintentional. She was still friends with Jess, and the two of them never spoke about it. It was just something in the past, which had stayed in the past, until today.
Avery simply nodded, "That's cool."

Chloe wasn't sure what she was anticipating, but it wasn't that reaction. The stress she had been unconsciously holding in her shoulders dropped away immediately. *I guess it's not really a big of a deal as I had thought,* Chloe thought to herself. *Fuck I'm here painting my nails with my metamour, of course she doesn't think it's weird I like girls too.* "What about you?" Chloe asked Avery.

"Five." Avery said, without having to think. "I've only ever kissed a girl though."

Chloe laughed, "You don't have to have sex with women if you don't want to."

"I know," Avery shrugged, smiling as she blew on her nails. "I think I do want to though, at least once."

Chloe didn't know what to say as she felt her stomach flip. *Oh no,* she thought to herself, glancing down to hide the flush coming to her face. *I have a crush on my boyfriend's girlfriend.*

Chapter 13

Shaking her head gently to let her hair fall loose, Chloe felt the gentle warmth of the sun on her skin. Eyes closed, she took a deep breath, and relaxed back into the sun lounger. It was Saturday, and she was in the small backyard at Ezra and Avery's place, which was how she had spent the past few Saturday afternoons. The space was a paved courtyard with a small garden running along the fence, a vine which produced small and fragrant white flowers partially covering the fence. Chloe was sure it was jasmine, but she also had very little knowledge about plants, so wouldn't bet any money on it. Avery was next to her, on her own sun lounger, quietly reading a thin romance novel. Her dark hair was piled on top of her head, held precariously with a clip, and large, round sunglasses were perched on her nose. She was wearing a short sundress, with the straps pulled down to allow for the sun to hit her shoulders evenly, but which also allowed the neckline to slip, revealing an almost indecent amount of cleavage. She was tapping one foot as she read, her tongue peeking out of her mouth in a look of concentration. Her dark skin seemed to almost have a gold sheen in the sun, but that might just have been her sun lotion. Breathing in deeply, Chloe could smell the small white flowers on the fence, the coconut scent of Avery's lotion, and the sugary sweetness of the Moscato in her hand. In this moment, everything felt still, calm and perfect. *If I could lay here for the rest of my life I would*, she thought to herself. *And I would die a happy woman.*

It had been six weeks now since she had first come over to hang out with Avery, who had invited her back the next weekend, and the next, until now it was sort of a running date between the two. An entirely friendly date, with no further mention of their shared attraction for women. When she had arrived today, Ezra was getting ready for another date with Mel, this time going to meet her fiancé, Brad. Chloe had got to witness him flustering around the house, changing shirts multiple times, and asking for the opinions of Avery and herself. She thought it was adorable, watching a man she was now comfortably dating seem so flustered. Chloe grinned a little to herself imagining him being the same way before his date with her a couple of months ago. Chloe was quite enjoying spending time just with Avery, they had a lot more in common that she and Ezra did, and conversation came easily to the two of them. They were becoming good friends, possibly even best friends, which is exactly the dynamic Chloe wanted for her metamour. Even now, just sitting next to each other in the backyard, Chloe felt at ease. The silence was comfortable.

Suddenly, Avery snapped her book shut dramatically and sat up straight, the sudden noise making Chloe jump. The movement had caused her thick, dark hair to drop off the top of her head slightly, hanging awkwardly behind her. She removed her sunglasses and looked at Chloe with a grin, as Chloe heard Ezra's car pull into the driveway. Chloe sat upright too, placing her wine on the small table next to her, her hair falling forward over her chest. She had chosen to wear denim shorts today, with a fashionably frayed hem, and a cropped black singlet. She had been getting a lot of sun over these past few weekends with Avery, her pale skin erupting in an army of freckles, clearly visible now over her legs, arms, shoulder and chest. She swung her legs over the side of the chair as Avery put her book down behind her, slipping the straps of her sundress up effortlessly. Chloe stood, leaning forward to massage the imprint of the chair out from the back of her thighs. "Ah, that's the one bad thing about these chairs," Chloe said, the redness slowly fading. Avery glanced in her direction, and for a second Chloe thought she saw her dark eyes linger on her chest.

A metallic click sliced through the air, and Avery was looking towards the back gate which separated the yard and the carport. Chloe followed her gaze, dismissing it as her imagination. *Wishful thinking, probably.* Ezra swung the gate open, beaming, a bottle of wine under his arm. "Look at you both," he practically sung at them, his elation unmistakable. "Sitting out here like old friends."

Avery bounded over, her hair falling out completely as she strode towards Ezra and planted a kiss on his cheek. "Good date then?"

Ezra nodded, planting a deep kiss on Avery's lips. She reciprocated, the pair quickly melting into each other's arms. Chloe stood upright, her thighs having recovered, and picked up her glass of Moscato from the table, emptying the sweet liquid into her mouth in one go. It occurred to Chloe that this situation may have seemed strange for other people, maybe even her a few months ago, but since experiencing what it was like to be part of a healthy relationship for the first time, even if it was not exactly what she had expected, she couldn't have felt more comfortable. Avery was opening the back door of the house now, and Ezra looked over at Chloe, his eyes wandering up and down her sun kissed body. She felt that familiar lustful tingle she got whenever she was near him, and walked over, beaming. She really felt that she had discovered the perfect relationship.

"How are you today, cutie?" Ezra grinned, slipping his hand around Chloe's waist as she met him with a soft kiss. His beard was soft, and smelled faintly like the fragrant oil he used regularly. He must have put it though that morning before his date with the new girl.

"Great," she said, leaning her head against his bicep. He smiled down at her, his eyes shining. Chloe's heart was so full of happiness, she felt like she was walking on air. She lifted her head, and Ezra pushed her playfully towards the back door. She giggled, and walked though, a playful bounce in her step. She entered the small living area, eyes adjusting from being outside, and saw Avery exiting the kitchen with a plate of spring rolls and dip, gin in hand. Relaxing in the sun, Chloe had completely forgot they had put those in the oven. Ezra followed her in, letting the flyscreen door shut behind him, and slipped his hands seductively around Chloe's hips from behind. She felt his breath on her neck as he pushed himself against her, grunting softly as his crotch connected gently with her butt. She let out an involuntary squeak of surprise, and Ezra laughed, as he headed towards the couch to grab a spring roll.

"I'm keen for a drink," he said, mouth full. "Avery is set, Chloe, want some of this wine?"
"Sure," she said, heading to sit down with her polycule – another word she had found in her research. The group of people connected by partners. The word still felt a bit strange to her, but she loved that there was a term for what they were. She sat on the L-shaped couch, next to Avery, so she could reach the snacks easily. Ezra left for the kitchen, and a comfortable silence fell over the two women.

Mouth full of food, Avery was flicking through films, finally settling on one Chloe hadn't seen before. She turned it down so it wouldn't interrupt the conversation, and turned to look at Chloe. Touching her lightly on the cheek, her soft rosy lips parted into a soft smile "You've got a bit of sunburn there."

Chloe's heart jumped as she was suddenly struck with a warm feeling flooding her body from her chest to the tips of her fingers and toes. Avery's dark eyes glimmered as she blinked her long, thick lashes, and turned to look towards the kitchen, where Ezra was returning.

For a moment, Chloe sat, stunned. *Is Avery flirting with me?* She shook her head, maybe it was just from being out in the sun for so long. Before she could think too much about it though, Ezra was handing her a glass of white wine, and flopping onto the couch with a sigh.

All three of them sat on the couch for hours, chatting, and laughing. Ezra placed his arm around Chloe, and she snuggled in to him, the warmth of his embrace making her feel safe. She couldn't wipe the smile off her face, she was so happy in that moment. She looked up at Ezra, his soft beard brushing her forehead gently, and he too, was smiling. He slipped his hand down behind her to give her butt a tight squeeze, which made her body respond.

"Why don't we play a game?" Avery chimed in, looking at her phone. "I found a list of questions for *Never have I Ever*."

Chloe shrugged, "I guess so. Is this a drinking game?"

Avery nodded. "Yes, every time you *have* done something, take a sip."

Chloe righted herself, reaching for her glass. Ezra was chuckling to himself. "Oh man, this isn't going to be very fair for me."

"I don't know," Avery looked at Chloe cheekily. "You might be surprised."

Sitting up straight she cleared her throat, reading from her phone screen with her glass in her hand. "Never have I ever had sex."

All three studiously sipped their drinks.

"Never have I ever had sex in a car."

Just Chloe and Avery sipped, and Ezra laughed. "I'm too freaking tall."

"Never have I ever been to Europe. Ugh!" Avery scoffed, aggressively scrolling through her phone. "These are lame!"

"I've got one." Ezra said. "Never have I ever had sex at work."

Nobody drank, and Ezra laughed. "Well, I thought about it."

Chloe playfully hit his arm, laughing.

"Ah!" Avery exclaimed. "Never have I ever had sex with someone of the same gender as me."

"Gay sex?" Ezra questioned, shaking his head.

Avery looked at Chloe, raising her eyebrows. Chloe sheepishly drank, which caused Ezra to audibly gasp. "Really?!"

"Yeah," Chloe said. It felt surprisingly freeing to reveal something she had kept close to her chest for years. "Not a big deal, I had a girlfriend for a few months in high school."

Ezra nodded, but his eyes were dropped, eyeing her body. Chloe felt that familiar flutter of arousal.

"So, what, are you bisexual then?" Ezra asked curiously.

"I don't know," Chloe said, shrugging, feeling a bit awkward. "I guess? I just like who I like."

There was a pause, while Ezra studied Chloe's face. She would have given anything to have been able to hear what he was thinking in that moment. His lips pursed, and he looked her up and down, almost as if he was seeing her for the first time. She wasn't sure why, but the idea made her feel a bit uncomfortable.

"Never have I ever," Avery continued. "Had sex in the shower."

Avery sipped her drink, as Chloe and Ezra raised their eyebrows at her. She giggled, "What? Callum has a really nice shower."

Ezra fixed his eyes on Chloe with a sudden intensity. "Never have I ever had a threesome."

Chloe shook her head, as Avery looked at him knowingly. Nobody drank.

"Never have I ever wanted to." He continued, downing the rest of his drink without breaking eye contact with Chloe. His eyes were intense with passion, and Chloe felt her stomach flip. *Was he proposing we have a threesome?* She looked over at Avery, who met her eye. Chloe took in the sight of Avery fully, tanned legs sprawled on the couch under her sundress, the smell of lotion and fruity shampoo filling the room. Her rosy lips were parted into a cheeky smile, her dark eyes framed by heavy, thick lashes. Chloe felt a tinge of excitement. Yes, she was very attracted to Avery. She was stunning, but more than that, she was warm, inviting, kind and friendly. She was gorgeous to the core.

Avery glanced over at Ezra, who was staring at Chloe. He blinked, turning to look at Avery expectantly. She looked Chloe dead in the eye, the intensity of it making her heart beat loudly in her ears. Slowly, Avery lifted her glass to her lips and sipped.

Holy shit, Chloe thought, her body being flooded with lustful excitement so quickly she almost lost her balance. Without a second though, she threw the rest of her wine into her mouth and moved towards Avery.

Avery's kiss was soft, her hands running through Chloe's hair, passionate and gentle. She leaned forward to meet Chloe, her chest rising up against Chloe's as she inhaled in excitement. It took a moment for Chloe to register fully that she was kissing Avery, her soft lips tasting like a mixture of the tart tonic water from her drink, and the sweet strawberry flavour of her lip gloss. Chloe's heart began to beat faster, a wave of exhilaration crashing down, her entire body being stripped of all inhibitions. Chloe ran her hand up

Avery's neck to cup her head, her mouth opening slightly as they kissed with an ever-increasing passion. Chloe was overwhelmed with excitement, her mind becoming focused only on Avery, the slight floral scent of her hair and the softness of her skin against her own.

A large, rough hand slid around Chloe's waist, and beard hairs tickled her neck as Ezra began kissing it from behind her. She jumped slightly at his touch, having forgotten he was there while she was engrossed in Avery. She leaned back into him, her heart pounding loudly in her ears, as Avery pulled her sundress up and over her head. Her dark hair fell across her bare shoulders as she cast the dress aside, her thick lashes batting as she lifted her eyes to meet Chloe's. For a moment, Chloe was stuck staring at Avery, and she couldn't help but think she was the most beautiful person she had ever seen. There was nothing, absolutely nothing, about her which was not perfect in Chloe's eyes. Ezra's hands slipped beneath Chloe's shirt, pushing the fabric up and over her head. Chloe turned to look at Ezra as he removed his own shirt quickly, and grabbed Chloe's face with both his hands, enveloping her is a passionate kiss. This was the most excited Chloe had ever seen Ezra, full of frantic energy.

Avery had unclasped her bra in this time, and let it fall to the floor as Chloe turned back to face her. Her breasts were full and perky, softly filling Chloe's hands. Chloe couldn't take her eyes off the soft peach colour of her nipples as Avery moved forward to kiss Chloe once more. Taking Chloe's face in her hands, Avery kissed her gently, her hands caressing over her back as the searched for Chloe's bra clasp. Chloe began to kiss Avery's neck, her soft breasts brushing against her chest, almost like velvet. She let out an involuntary moan as she lifted her hand to cup Avery's breast gently. Avery let out a slight whimper, and faltered in her efforts to undo Chloe's bra, as Chloe took both of Avery's breasts in her hands, gently applying pressure, and lowering herself to kiss one of her nipples. Avery bit her lip, moaning quietly, and Chloe continued, sensually kissing and sucking on Avery's nipple, as Avery's eyelids fluttered in arousal. Chloe could feel herself becoming incredibly wet as she tended to Avery, the beautiful woman melting like putty in her hands.

Chloe could hear Ezra behind her unclasping his belt and removing his jeans, but was too engrossed with the goddess in front of her to pay much mind. Avery had abandoned the clasp of Chloe's bra and was leaning back into the couch, one of her hands moving to support her own head, and one to Chloe's hair. Her delicate fingers moving across Chloe's scalp felt incredibly intimate, and Chloe pushed her body closer to Avery's, moving between her slender thighs. Ezra brushed past her, out of her line of sight as she switched to the other nipple, a fresh gasp of exhilaration escaping Avery's lips. Chloe looked up as she heard Ezra grunt, to see his cock, bulging and erect, in Avery's small hand. Her face turned towards him, and she looked up at him with her dark eyes, opened her supple lips and guided the head of his cock into her mouth.

Ezra's head tiled back as he moaned with ecstasy. He thrust his cock into her mouth, and Avery moaned with enjoyment as she began to work his shaft. Chloe looked up at Ezra's face as he looked back down at Avery, his mouth hanging open as he breathed heavily. Her heart was pounding in her ears as she slid her hands down over Avery's soft stomach, slipping her fingers into the waistband of her underwear and removing them. Avery lifted her hips to help, expertly continuing to suck and lick Ezra's cock. Chloe now found herself between Avery's naked thighs, her neatly shaved pussy in front of her, the juices making it glisten slightly in the living room light. Chloe had not been in this position for a very long time, and never with her partner preoccupied like this. Her excitement became nervousness as she gently stroked Avery's inner thighs. She ran her thumb over Avery's lips and she inhaled sharply with excitement, hips tilting towards Chloe eagerly. Any trepidation she had felt immediately evaporated as she began to stroke Avery, the other woman responding with her own heavy breathing and moans. Before too long Avery let out a whimper, and pulled her head back from Ezra's cock, turning to face Chloe. Her face was twisted into a look Chloe knew too well, her short and sharp breaths exciting Chloe to continue her rhythm, while Avery squeaked, and, holding her breath, threw her head back.

Chloe's confidence soared, having seen Avery enjoy her touch so much, and slipped two fingers inside Avery's wet opening. Her heart was pounding in her ears as she moved her body closer to Avery, the beautiful woman seeming to melt with her touch. Chloe lowered her lips to Avery's entrance, gently kissing her. Avery let out a muffled cry, and Chloe continued, sucking and licking Avery's wetness as she fingered her. Soon Avery's panting became rhythmic, and she began to hold her breath. Chloe felt her muscles contracting around her fingers as she came, hard. Chloe responded, eagerly kissing and licking at Avery's pussy, removing her fingers so she could stay balanced as Avery shuddered and shook beneath her.

Chloe pulled back from Avery for a moment, the sweet taste of her on her lips. Avery was lying back on the couch, her naked tanned skin shimmering slightly with sweat. Her full chest was rising and falling rhythmically as she panted, recovering from her orgasm. Her eyes were closed, her rosy lips forming a slight smile, her dark hair in a pool around her head. Chloe kissed her stomach, her heart soaring as she touched Avery's soft skin. She really was the most beautiful woman she had ever seen.

Reaching back to unclasp her bra, Chloe adjusted her position in between Avery's thighs. She let her breasts fall with a slight bounce as she cast her bra aside. Avery opened her eyes, her dark lashed fluttering as she met Chloe's gaze, and smiled softly. Chloe's heart seemed to leap into her throat, and the rest of the world seemed to fall away. Chloe lowered her face back between Avery's legs, and gently kissed her clit, Avery responding with a sharp inhale. Chloe continued, slower and softer this time, lavishing the way Avery responded to her touches.

Broad hands slipped around Chloe's waist, and she could feel Ezra unbuttoning her shorts, and sliding them down over her thigh, taking her underwear with them. Chloe shifted her weight slightly to help him, fully focused on pleasuring Avery. Naked now, she felt Ezra's hands stroking her hips, shifting her so she was on her knees. His hands slid between her thighs, searching for her opening, a deep moan escaping him when he discovered just how excited she was. He traced over her lips with his thumb, a shiver running through her body. Next thing she knew, she could feel his beard on her legs as he began to kiss and lick her pussy too. Chloe moaned gently, insanely aroused at the realisation that she was now at the centre of their affections, her excitement fuelling her servicing of Avery. It was more difficult now to keep any sort of rhythm, as Ezra was causing her to pant, tremble and moan herself. Chloe's excitement was building, as was Avery's, the two women heaving together with their gentle moans.

Avery wrapped her legs around Chloe's shoulders, pulling her deeper into her. Chloe felt Avery pushing against her, her excitement building. Ezra's broad hands were caressing her thighs and ass as he ate her out, occasionally firmly squeezing her thighs. Ezra's thumb teased its way across Chloe's glistening lips, making her shudder with excitement. Ezra grunted, climbing to his knees behind her, as Avery's bucked her hips against Chloe's face, crying out as her body shuddered. Chloe was trapped for a moment between Avery's thighs, her sweet nectar running over her lips and chin. It was heaven.

Avery's body relaxed, and she lay back, gasping for air, her face breaking into a smile of pure joy. Chloe pulled up slightly, only to feel Ezra's hands wrap around her hips. Looking back, she saw him perched behind her, ready to enter her, his hungry gaze switching back and forth between the two women. Chloe grinned, and pushed herself back against his erect penis, which found her opening easily. She could feel her own juices dripping down her thighs as Ezra grunted, beginning to thrust back and forth into her. She was more aroused than she had ever been, and it felt like Ezra was too, with the enthusiasm he was pumping into her. She licked her lips as she pushed back against him, tasting Avery as she did, eager to cum herself. Ezra grunted rhythmically, his fingers digging into Chloe's soft hips. Her breathing quickened, and she tensed, at the precipice of her orgasm, when Avery grabbed her face roughly and kissed her deeply. Chloe came, and the world seemed to fade away around her as Avery's soft lips danced across hers. Ezra's fingers dug in to her as he held himself inside, feeling the pulse of her body against his cock. He moaned loudly, pumping twice and then stopping again, which caused Chloe to cry out.

"Fuck!" He shouted, before pounding hard and fast as he came, his grip so tight it almost hurt. He finished, and pulled out, throwing himself back onto the couch in obvious annoyance. Chloe collapsed forward onto her stomach, catching her breath. It was pretty clear that Ezra had not intended to finish so soon, but whether it was the sight of the two women together, or the intensity of Chloe's orgasm, or both, the threesome was over much sooner than he had intended.

There was a moment of silence as Chloe breathed, head resting on Avery's thigh, legs shaking. Turning her head, she could see Ezra on the couch, head leaning back, hands covering his face. She blinked, pushing herself upright. She opened her mouth to say something, but before she could make a sound, Avery's soft, delicate fingers slid onto her cheek. Chloe turned to face her, and was stunned by her big brown eyes. Avery smiled sweetly, before leaning in to kiss Chloe again. Her other hand traced up the back of Chloe's neck and into her messy hair, the passion of the kiss intensifying. Chloe gasped, melting into Avery's arms. Suddenly, Ezra stood up from the couch and charged out of the room, slamming the bedroom door behind him.

The two women froze, and Chloe looked at Avery, searching her expression. She was looking at the bedroom door, her face giving away her frustration. She turned back to Chloe, and dropped her hand from her head, pulling back. Chloe did the same, casting her eyes down as she awkwardly gathered up her things and got dressed again. Without a word, she headed towards the door.

"Chloe," Avery started, and Chloe stopped dead, looking back at the beautiful, naked woman on the couch. For a moment the two locked eyes, and Chloe's heart swelled. She wanted to say something profound, something apologetic, or something useful. Nothing came to her. She managed a tight lipped smile before she left, the heavy wooden door closing behind her with a resounding thud.

Chapter 14

Chloe was poking her fork around her plate, barely touching the salad she had prepared for lunch. She glanced down at her phone. *Nothing,* she sighed. She had been desperately waiting for a message since she had left their house over the weekend, but had received only radio silence. She wanted to say something to them, but what? She wasn't entirely sure she understood what had happened.

Tucking a loose strand of hair behind her ear distractedly, Chloe glanced around the busy lunch room. She was sure that this relationship with Ezra, and with Avery, was over. Somehow, in that threesome, she had messed up, and they no longer wanted to see her.

Just then, Ezra entered through the doors, and strolled towards the fridge. Her heart flipped, partially in excitement, but mostly in fear this time. This was the first time she had seen him since he had stormed out of the room. She watched carefully as he placed his food in the microwave and pressed the button to reheat, leaning back against the bench with his arms crossed casually. She was attempting to read his mood from his movements, but she couldn't discern anything. Then, he looked straight at her, their eyes locking across the room.

Chloe couldn't quite read his expression, it was mostly blank, but there was a flicker of something in his eyes. She looked back down at her food quickly as heat rushed to her face. She hated this feeling, like she had done something wrong, but had no idea what it was. Her brain was desperately spinning, trying to work it out so she could apologise and make everything right again. Next thing she knew, the plastic container was being placed on the table with a gentle clunk, and Ezra's broad body slid into the chair opposite her.

Chloe realised she was holding her breath, and took a moment to focus on her breathing, staring desperately at her salad. Her heart was racing, and she was doing everything in her power to try and look composed, but her deep breaths were drawing in that familiar cologne that made her stomach tighten. Ezra hadn't moved, hadn't said anything. She looked up at him, and his face wore an expression of genuine concern.

"Chloe," he said softly in his rumbling baritone. "Are you okay?"

Chloe began to nod, but as she did, her chest tightened and her eyes welled involuntarily. She looked away, desperately trying to hold back the tears that were now falling uncontrollably from her eyes. She realised she had readied herself for the worst, but was completely unprepared for Ezra to still care about her.

"Hey," Ezra reached out and grabbed her hand in his. Shocked, she looked back at him. This was the polar opposite of what she had been expecting. "Chloe, what's wrong?"

She shook her head, trying desperately to not be completely overcome by the intensity of her feelings. She was sure that if she opened her mouth to speak, it would open the flood gates. *I'm right back there again,* she thought to herself. *I'm acting crazy.* She took a deep breath and looked right at Ezra. No, he was the one who needed to explain himself.

"You tell me." She whispered at him, it coming out harsher than she had intended to.

Ezra's face washed with understanding, and his shoulders dropped. He reached for her other hand, holding it in his across the table. This was the most intimate he had ever been with her at work, right in the middle of the lunch room. Taking a deep breath, he opened her mouth to speak, but nothing came out. Instead, he squeezed her hands gently.

Suddenly, the reality of where they were hit them both at the same time. The two of them made a panicked eye contact, as they realised they had completely dropped the façade of "just friends" they had at work. Ezra released her hands and pulled his arms down by his side. The two went back to poking at their lunches. Chloe felt a soft smile creep across her face as she chewed on her salad. He wasn't furious at her. The relationship wasn't over. The weight of those thoughts lifted, she now started to bubble with curiosity. *How dare he make me feel that way?* She thought, angrily.

After a couple of moments of silence, Chloe looked up at Ezra, who was staring intently at his food, seemingly lost in thought. She remembered the first day she had seen him, and not been attracted at all. The man with dishevelled hair had become the man she couldn't stop thinking about. Now, she was living a life she had never even dreamed possible. Tilting her head to the side as she chewed, she studied him, searching for any sign of a reason for his behaviour the other day. He sat up straight, glancing around the room, brow furrowed. His expression was serious, but his eyes slightly glassy, as if he couldn't really see the room though the heaviness of his thoughts.

Ezra met her gaze for a moment, and after shovelling the rest of his food in his mouth, nodded his head towards the side entrance to the lunch room. *Ah, maybe I will get an explanation after all,* she thought. He stood, and walked towards the door. Trying her best to look calm, Chloe followed suit, making a conscious effort not to look like she was rushing to put her things away.

Walking into the hallway, Chloe was only a few meters behind Ezra, who opened the door to the stairwell. His expression was stern. Stepping in, he let the door swing shut behind him. As Chloe reached the door, heart pounding in her ears, nervous about the conversation they were about to have, she paused and took a deep breath to steady herself. She pushed the door open, and entered the small landing.

Immediately the cool air with that familiar damp smell hit her nostrils. Something about it made her feel like she was deep underground. She crossed her arms across her body as she stepped in, letting the door close with a soft thud behind her.

Ezra was standing in the corner, leaning against the wall, eyes cast down at his shoes. His hands were in his pockets and he was shuffling his foot nervously.

"Chloe," he said, softly. "I am so sorry for the way I behaved. I—" he looked up at her and their eyes met for just a second. Warmth rushed through her as she realised what was happening. Every fibre of her body was urging her to stop him from apologising, to somehow take the blame herself, but she fought it. Standing there silently, her fingers gripping her arms to steady herself, she waited to hear what he had to say.

Ezra looked down, and laughed a little. "I was actually really disappointed to see that you had gone. You know, once I stopped being mad at myself."

Chloe nodded, a small laugh escaping her mouth. She swallowed, suddenly very aware of how dry her mouth was. *What do I even say to that?* She shook her head, "I thought—"

Ezra lifted his hand to stop her, levelling her with a steady gaze. "You thought wrong, babe."

Chloe nodded, annoyance flickering across her face as she looked down, and they stood in silence for a moment. Part of her was mad at him for cutting her off like that, and dismissing what she had to say, but most of her was relieved that he hadn't blamed her for everything and broken up with her. It was just one of those little things that annoyed her about Ezra, the way he cut her off sometimes. It made her feel like he wasn't really listening to her. *But, nobody is perfect, right?* She thought with resignation. *I'm certainly not.*

She was looking everywhere but at Ezra. At the dusty floor, the roughly textured walls. She could hear the fluorescent light humming in the silence. Overwhelmingly, she felt stupid for blaming herself. "Ezra, I'm sorry." She said, tears brimming in her eyes. "I shouldn't have run away."

Ezra righted himself and walked over to her, embracing her in a solid hug. "No, you have nothing to be sorry for." He said, his deep voice echoing slightly in the concrete room. "I just—" his voice caught for a moment, and he squeezed her tighter. "I finished too quickly. It wasn't what I wanted and I just... I didn't know how to handle it except to get mad."

Chloe pressed her face into his chest, waiting for him to continue. His cologne was faint now, being the middle of the day, but she could still smell it on his clothes. She took a deep breath, trying to inhale enough of it to give her that tingly feeling in her stomach.

"I built it up in my head you know, the fantasy," he continued. "And then it didn't go how I expected, and it was entirely on me." He sighed. "I'm so sorry I made you feel like anything was your fault, Chloe. I wasn't thinking about how it would make you and Avery feel."

Relief washed over Chloe. Suddenly, she felt ridiculous, her face flushing red with embarrassment. *I did nothing wrong at all,* she said, feeling a bit insane for ever thinking it was her fault at all. Luckily, she was still being held by Ezra, so he didn't notice. He gave her a gentle squeeze as they stood in silence, and planted a gentle kiss on the top of her head. *I feel so stupid for running off like I did,* she thought. Chloe couldn't help it, but she felt like she owed it to Ezra to try again. *I want to make him happy.* She affirmed in her own mind. *Because I care about him.*

"Ezra," Chloe said, stepping back to look at him. "I really am sorry that it didn't go the way that you hoped. Maybe—" He opened his mouth to say something, but Chloe levelled him with a stare which indicated she wasn't finished speaking. He smiled as he closed his mouth. Sometimes he got it right. "Maybe we could try it again?"

His eyes lit up. "Really?"

Chloe struggled to contain a giggle. "Yeah, I'd really like to."

Ezra grabbed her face and pulled her lips to meet his, his beard tickling her face. Chloe melted into the kiss, all the tension leaving her body. She was good, they were good, everything was good. She couldn't help but feel a feeling of content happiness coming over her. For a moment, she wondered how she ever got by in life without this kind of relationship. Polyamory was really the lifestyle for her.

Gently, Ezra lifted his head, clearing his throat. Chloe had noticed the bulge in his pants becoming harder against her body. "Sorry," he said softly. "Kind of difficult to control the thing when you talk about having a threesome." He looked at her with a slight smile, stroking the side of her face with the back of his hand. "You're not just saying that are you?"

Chloe shrugged, pushing herself against him so that her body pressed up against his growing bulge. "No," she whispered, leaning into him. "I'd have sex with you any day, Ezra." *And Avery too,* she thought, mind wandering back to her soft skin, her deep brown eyes, her gentle kiss.

He grunted softly, eyes closing for just a second. She leaned up to kiss him, on her tiptoes, and he kissed her back, enthusiastically. He was starting to breathe heavily when she stepped back, tracing her finger down his chest. She tilted her head with a cheeky grin, trying to be coy. "Plus, your girlfriend is super hot."

Ezra burst out laughing, his booming voice echoing in the concrete stairwell before he clasped a hand to his mouth, realising the noise he was making. *Maybe someone heard that?* The thought crossed Chloe's mind fleetingly, but surprisingly she felt no pang of fear or anxiety about it. Her mind was wandering, thinking of what she could do with Ezra right now in the secluded stairwell with that hard cock.

She stepped towards him with a mischievous grin, but he checked his watch and stood bolt upright. "Shit, I've got a meeting in five minutes." He cleared his throat, and Chloe stepped back. She had almost forgot they were at work. He straightened out his shirt, and attempted to hide his obvious erection in the belt of his pants with a frustrated sigh. Looking at Chloe hungrily, he smiled. "What are you doing Friday night?"

She grinned, seeing the opportunity to be cheeky. "Hopefully you."

He threw his head back, smiling, a frustrated grunt echoing in the stairwell. Chloe couldn't help but laugh at herself. She shrugged. "I'll leave first then." Ezra nodded, still trying to calm down.

Chloe pushed the door open and stepped into the hallway, slipping out silently and walking back towards the office where her desk was. Just then, Carla came out of the ladies' bathroom, which was in the same hallway. "Chloe!" she said, her face breaking into a smile. "I missed you at lunch today."

"Ah," Chloe said, her brain racing to try and find an excuse. "I was just—"

Just then, the door to the stairwell opened, and Ezra stepped out. Chloe's heart dropped out of her chest as Carla's eyes widened in shock. Ezra looked at both women for a long moment in silence, expression deadpan. Nobody spoke. *Oh shit,* Chloe thought, eyes wide and jaw clenched. The Ezra nodded, turned on his heels and walked briskly down the hallway in the opposite direction.
Chloe tried to walk past Carla, but her hand grabbed her arm, her grip a little firmer than necessary. "Chloe!" she whispered. "Did you and Ezra just-?"

"No." Chloe said, annoyed, and trying to shrug free of her friend's grip. "We were just talking."

Carla raised her eyebrows at Chloe. "Seriously," Chloe said, raising her eyebrows back.

Carla let go of her friend's arm and folded hers. "Okay, but what did you have to talk about, which was so secretive, you had to go in the stairwell?" Her mouth twisted into a smile. "Unless this isn't the first time you've seen Ezra behind closed doors?"

Chloe smiled sarcastically at her friend, and Carla's jaw dropped. Chloe walked away, back to her desk, holding her breath the entire way. She wasn't sure if her friend was more surprised by the revelation that she was seeing Ezra, or by her attitude, but in that moment, she didn't particularly care. She wasn't sure what had come over her, but suddenly she felt a confidence in herself she had never really felt before. And it felt amazing.

Chapter 15

Chloe knocked on the solid wood door, noticing how still and quiet the street was this evening. There was a slight chill to the air as a breeze tickled past her exposed calves, and she shivered. Holding her denim jacket close to her, she wished she had worn jeans. *It's only going to get colder later.* The door opened, and Ezra stood there, in his standard denim jeans and plain black tee. He smiled and stepped to the side to let her in. Chloe walked by, the coolness of the breeze outside forgotten as her heart started to beat faster and her face flushed with warmth. The door closed, and she felt Ezra's broad hands immediately snake their way beneath her skirt, cupping her butt. He leaned in close to her and kissed her neck, Chloe sighing with pleasure. It was so nice to feel wanted after a long week of stressful and repetitive work.

Avery appeared from around the corner, her long hair loose about her shoulders, wearing an oversize jumper and leggings. Her face broke into a beaming smile when she saw Chloe, and she bounded forward to give her a hug. Chloe couldn't help but grin. Avery wrapped her arms around her and playfully pushed Ezra away. "Hey, we need to eat dinner first!" she laughed.

"Do we though?" he grinned through his complaint, his voice teasing. "We could eat after."

"There's a joke in here somewhere about you just eating me," Chloe said, beaming cheekily. Ezra burst into laughter and Avery raised her eyebrows as she started to giggle.

"Fuck," Ezra said, wiping tears from his eyes. "I was not expecting that."

Avery waved her phone, which she had been holding in her hand. "Seriously though, let's get this pizza order in."

Ezra breezed past Chloe, gently kissing Avery on the forehead as he took the phone from her. Flopping onto the couch with a thud, he scrolled through the phone to make his selection.

Chloe and Avery made eye contact, and Chloe felt her heart flip. Avery smiled sweetly, tucking her hair behind her ear as she turned away, joining Ezra on the couch. Putting her bag down near the door, Chloe chuckled to herself. The thought of being back here, after what happened last time, had made her tremble with nerves. It was the feeling that would have made the old Chloe run for the hills, but she was determined to push through it. She wanted more than anything for this to work out. "You like pepperoni, right?" Ezra shouted back at Chloe.

"Yep." She replied, joining them on the couch with a smile. "You remembered."

Ezra shrugged, smiling. After a few more taps on the phone he dropped it onto the coffee table and leant back into the cushions. Avery on his right, hair falling loose over the throw cushions, and Chloe on his left, in her knee length sundress and denim jacket. He looked back and forth for a moment, his face stuck in a wide grin. "I can't believe this is my life. Honestly."

Chloe smiled, looking over at Avery, who was watching Ezra with adoring eyes. The sun was filtering through the sheer curtains, giving her hair a slight caramel glow. Chloe's heart was in her throat as she thought about kissing Avery's soft brown neck.

Avery adjusted her seating position so she was sitting straight on the couch, clearing her throat as she did so. "Okay," she levelled Chloe with a serious look. "We are going to have a talk about this whole thing now. Get everything out in the air so there is no more second guessing, no more doubt about what we are doing."

Chloe nodded, shifting her weight so she was sitting forward attentively. She licked her lips nervously, but Avery made it sound so non-threatening, she wasn't at all terrified. *This is what adults do, right?* Chloe thought to herself. *They communicate.*

Ezra nodded, looking straight ahead. "I'll start," he said, his voice determined.

Chloe and Avery were both looking at him expectantly, but Ezra was silent. He seemed to be thinking, perhaps choosing his words carefully. Chloe could see from the encouraging expression on Avery's face that she had a fair idea of what he was about to say.

"I want to apologise to you both for the way I acted," he said. "It was selfish and immature. I am going to do my best to do better." He turned his head to look at Avery. "You know how much I love you, and how I would do anything for you, babe." She nodded, smiling. "I want to be the best version of myself at all times because that's who you deserve to be with." She grabbed his hand and gave it a squeeze while they shared eye contact. Avery leaned in and planted a gentle kiss on Ezra's lips. Then he turned to Chloe.

His eyes were shimmering, looking like deep pools of honey in the dappled light from the curtains. Chloe's heart flipped, and she swallowed nervously. He was leaning towards her, and placed his broad hand on her thigh. She felt her body tingle with involuntary arousal, and his mouth slipped into a smile. He leaned forward. "Chloe."

She swallowed, nodding. How was he able to make her feel this way, even after all this time? Ezra moved his other hand to brush the hair away from her face as he continued. "I know I've already told you, but I want to say it again. I am sorry for the way I behaved. And I am especially sorry that you felt like you were to blame."

He leant in, planting a gentle and sensual kiss on her lips. She could feel his body press against hers, pulling her in. He leaned back, levelling her with a serious look. His hand was on her chin, cupping her face. She could hear her heart beating in her ears, as she felt her entire body melt into jelly. Ezra smiled, his eyes twinkling with happiness.
 "Chloe, I love you."

Chloe's mouth fell open, her stomach flipped, she blinked her eyes a few times. She was not expecting that. Suddenly a panic washed over her, as she realised she didn't feel the same.

"Ezra—" she managed, before he lifted a finger to her lips to keep her from continuing.
"I just wanted you to know," he said. "You don't have to say it back."
He must have been able to see it written all over her face. Silently she cursed herself for being so transparent, but her stomach tightened in annoyance at him cutting her off again. She nodded,

looking down at the couch. *Nobody is perfect, Chloe.* She told herself. *He wants you, and finds you attractive, despite everything. That should be enough for you.* But, it wasn't.

He leant in for a quick kiss before throwing himself back onto the cushions with a sigh of relief, and turning to Avery.
"So babe, what did you want to say?"

Avery nodded, looking from Ezra to Chloe. "Chloe," her voice caught in her throat. She looked downwards, and adjusted herself in the chair. "Chloe, I have never found women attractive before." She started, still looking down. "But you—" She cut herself off, and looked up at Chloe. Her hair tumbled over her shoulders as tears brimmed in her eyes. Chloe had never seen her look so emotional and raw. She couldn't help but be struck by how stunning she was in that moment.

"Chloe, I am so attracted to you. To who you are as a person, as well as physically. I think about you when you aren't here, and it makes my heart flutter. I guess what I'm trying to say is, I really like you and enjoy your company. I want you to be around more than you aren't. And I want you to feel comfortable and safe here with us."

Chloe was lost for words. Her heart felt like it was going to explode out of her chest. She swallowed, nodding. *Holy hell,* she thought. *What do I even say now?*

"You are both wonderful," she managed, grinning from ear to ear. "I'm sorry... I wasn't expecting this."

Avery nodded, wiping her eyes. "I figure if we are going to keep this relationship together, we need to communicate." Chloe nodded in agreement.

Ezra clasped his hands together and held them to his mouth, as if he was thinking of what to say. "In saying that," he started, very seriously. "It was my bad last time, not communicating my expectations and then reacting poorly. So, I would like to have a discussion about our expectations for tonight."

Chloe's eyes widened, but Avery nodded in agreement. He was right, it would be best if they were all on the same page, but she was so out of her depth right now. Her head was whirling. Talking about her expectations or wants before a sexual experience was completely foreign to her.
 Just then, there was a knock at the door, and Avery jumped up to answer.

"Pizza!" Ezra shouted gleefully, turning to Chloe with a smile. "Don't stress Chloe. There's no wrong answers."

She nodded, relaxing into herself. Chloe shook her head, smiling nervously. "I've never done this before. You know, talked about something before it happens."

Ezra nodded. "Yeah it's new for us too." He leaned forward to place a hand on her thigh. It was reassuring, but also flirty. He smiled mischievously. "You know you're in a safe space here."

Chloe nodded, smiling, as Avery placed the pizza boxes on the table, and collapsed back into the couch with a laugh. "Pause that thought, pizza first."

Ezra laughed, leaning forward to check which pizza belonged to which person, and distributing them. Chloe was silent, opening the cardboard to reveal the steamy, cheesy dinner. Suddenly she realised just how hungry she was, and lifted the first piece from the box. So many thoughts were spinning in her head. *Pause those thoughts, Chloe.* She thought to herself, watching the cheese stretch and break as she lifted the piece to her mouth. *Pizza first.*

Chapter 16

Avery pushed the door open to the bedroom, turning her head to look at Chloe over her shoulder as she stepped through the threshold. Avery's fingers danced across Chloe's palm as she loosely held her hand. Chloe stepped in, the fruity smell of incense immediately hitting her nostrils. Avery dropped Chloe's hand and made her way to the bed, sitting near the pillows. This was just as they had discussed, so Chloe knew what to expect next. It was an incredibly freeing feeling.

Ezra's hands slid around her waist as he leaned in to kiss her neck, his chest pressing against her back. Chloe inhaled sharply as she felt her arousal increase. His hands moulded over her figure, feeling her hips, stomach and breasts. Chloe trembled, feeling herself melting to his touch. She couldn't believe this was real. It felt so slow, sensual. Perfect.

Ezra groaned softly behind her, so softly that if he had not been in her ear, she may not have heard him. Running his hands down over her thighs, he lifted her dress up and over her head, tossing it to the ground next to them. Then, he continued to caress her body, tracing over the edges of her bra and underwear teasingly. Chloe could feel his breath on her back and shoulders, could hear him becoming aroused as he did so.

Ezra placed one of his hands firmly between her shoulders, and gently pushed her forwards, indicating for her to bend over. Chloe obliged eagerly, placing her hands on the bed. Her brain had become fuzzy already, her pussy growing wetter with every passing

moment. There was a sliding noise as Ezra removed his leather belt from his jeans, and Chloe glanced back at him to see him folding it in half in his hands, his eyes trained intently on her ass.
The sound of the leather connecting with Chloe's skin was more of a shock in the quiet room than the stinging pain, but Chloe flinched nonetheless. Ezra bought the belt down across her again, on the other side now, and again she flinched as the leather connected. Smiling, Chloe could feel her adrenaline start to kick in now, and this one hurt less than the last. She looked up at Avery, who was relaxing into the pillows, her face broken into a wide smile. She was obviously enjoying herself.

Three more hits in quick succession, and it was too much for Chloe, who cried out and dropped herself to her side.

"Did I say you could roll over?" Ezra said, smiling. Chloe had always wanted to be spanked, so was more than happy to oblige. She was thrilled. The way he spoke to her now, with complete control, was really working for her. As her backside throbbed, and the stinging of the initial blow subsided, she rolled back to present him it to him again. She held her safe word in her mind, in case she needed it.

Ezra bought the belt down over her two more times, before Chloe rolled over, bringing her hands to her raw skin. It was hot to the touch, but it felt good to softly rub her palms over the marks.

Avery moved towards Ezra, pulling her dress up over her head and throwing it to the ground. Ezra made eye contact with Chloe, his face seeming to check she was okay, so she nodded, smiling. Nodding once in acknowledgement, he turned to Avery, dropping his belt on the floor and pulling his shirt up over his head. Avery expertly slipped her fingers into the waistband of his jeans, pulling him towards her, on all fours on the bed. Then, looking up at him, she unbuttoned his jeans and slips them down with his underwear to reveal his penis, fully erect. Licking her lips, she slid it in her mouth.

Ezra's head fell back as he moaned, one hand running through her dark hair as she slowly licked and sucked on his cock. Chloe, lying on her side and watching, took the opportunity to get naked, letting her bra and underwear fall to the floor. Ezra grabbed the back of Avery's head, looking down at her, and thrust into her mouth a handful of times, grunting softly, before she pulled back, gagging.

Avery sat back on her legs, removing her bra, and Ezra stepped out of his jeans, his penis rock hard. Ezra looked between the two women on the mattress, smiling eagerly. He placed a hand on Avery's thigh, "Come to the edge on the bed, on your knees." She immediately obliged, slipping her underwear off as she moved.

Avery gasped as Ezra entered her, her mouth dropping open deliciously as she made eye contact with Chloe. A shiver of arousal ran through her body as she watched Avery's face light up with pleasure, the soft sounds of Ezra's thrusting filling the room. Ezra was grunting, softly and deeply, both his hands hooked expertly around Avery's hips. Chloe adjusted herself on the bed so that she was in front of Avery, who was now moaning slightly, her body riding each thrust. Chloe was so transfixed by how beautiful Avery was in that moment, she was completely beyond any fear or nervousness. Confidently, she cupped Avery's chin and leaned in, passionately kissing her. Avery kissed back; her tongue desperate to meet Chloe's. Soon, Avery's moaning intensified, and she was unable to reciprocate the kiss, gasping for air as she came. She closed her eyes, her cries becoming louder, as Ezra grunted from behind her. He slowed, allowing her to ride out her orgasm gently, and then stepped back, wiping sweat from his face with a smile.

Avery collapsed onto her side, laughing as she gasped for air. Chloe leaned down to kiss her, Avery reaching up to cup her face as their lips touched. It was soft and sensual, completely different from kissing Ezra, and Chloe felt a warmth spread through her as she smiled. She pulled back from the kiss, Avery's dark eyes shimmering like pools of rich honey, the floral smell of her hair filling Chloe's nostrils and sending a shiver through her. Chloe ran her hands over Avery's body, her tanned skin soft and warm beneath her fingers. Avery inhaled as Chloe gently cupped her breast, fingers teasing gently over her nipple. Hearing Avery reacting to her touch like that thrilled Chloe, who cupped the back of Avery's head and kissed her, passionately, increasing the vigour of her touch. Avery moaned as Chloe played with her nipple, moving to kiss her neck.

Ezra's hand ran up Chloe's leg, following the natural curve of her body, until it lingered on her ass. As Chloe kissed Avery's neck, she felt Ezra slide his hand to her thigh, before pulling her to the edge to the bed. His grip was firm and forceful, and Chloe slid across the sheets easily. She laughed, and looked up at Ezra, standing above her. He was glistening with sweat, his hair falling over his face slightly, but his eyes hungry as he pushed himself up next to her. Running the head of his cock over her opening, Chloe inhaled with excitement. Then, he pushed into her, the full length of him making her whimper with pleasure.

Avery had moved down the bed too, and was kissing Chloe's nipples, her tongue dancing expertly over Chloe's pale skin, making her shudder. Ezra soon got into a rhythm, and Chloe was soon cumming, her body pushing against him as she did, soft cries escaping her mouth. She found herself gripping Avery's soft hair in her fist as she rode her orgasm, with Avery moaning as she did. Ezra was above them, grunting, sweat dripping from his forehead, down onto Chloe's stomach as he thrusted. He slowed, and looked at Avery, who met his gaze with a mischievous and knowing smile. Turning to Chloe, Avery tilted her head and blinked her heavy lashes. "Can I sit on your face?"

"Please", Chloe begged breathlessly, without even thinking. Ezra stepped back, his broad hands resting on Chloe's knees as Avery effortlessly swung her thigh over Chloe's head, to face Ezra. Immediately, Chloe was struck by just how smooth Avery's legs were on either side of her head, her skin smelling faintly of cocoa butter. Her pussy was there, just above Chloe's face, the juices all but dripping from it. Avery leaned forward, kissing Ezra, as her pussy hovered tantalisingly above Chloe's face. Chloe placed her hands on Avery's perky buttocks, enjoying the softness of her skin as she gently leaned back. Eagerly, Chloe lifted her mouth to meet Avery's wetness, the sweet taste filling her mouth immediately. Avery made a soft noise as she pushed back into Chloe, almost riding her face. Flicking her tongue against Avery's clit, Chloe focused on listening to her moans, feeling her legs twitch, getting Avery to climax on her face. Chloe could feel herself becoming aroused too, feel her own juices gently dripping down her thigh. Avery's moans changed, became short and sharp, which spurred Chloe on, eager get Avery there. Before she knew it, Avery's thighs tensed on either side of her head, her hips twitched, and she whimpered, pussy dripping sweet juices into her mouth and over her chin as Avery orgasmed.

Avery leaned forward, catching her breath, and Chloe could hear Ezra kiss her. Although she couldn't see him from her position, Chloe felt Ezra's broad hand on her thigh, as Ezra pushed up against her, his cock sliding effortlessly into her again. She gasped, he felt somehow bigger than before, but that might just be because she

was already so aroused. Ezra lifted one of Chloe's legs to his shoulder, leaning into his thrusts, which were hitting deep inside Chloe, making her shudder with pleasure. Her hands still on Avery's thighs, she gripped her soft skin, and Avery looked back at her, a cheeky glint in her eye, as she moved her hips back, offering her pussy to Chloe's mouth once again. Without a thought Chloe lifted her head to meet it, the delicious taste of her juices sending her wild. The sounds of the three of them all softly grunting and moaning filling the room, Chloe was quickly getting close to orgasm. Ezra reached under her with one hand to grab her ass, and Chloe felt herself tipping over the edge. She had to pull away from Avery as she came, her body shuddering with the intensity. As she cried out between Avery's thighs, Ezra and Avery leant in to kiss above her. Ezra must have felt the intensity of her orgasm, because he pulled back from the kiss, groaning the loudest Chloe had ever heard him. "Fuck, oh fuck."
He grabbed Chloe as his whole body tensed, his cock filling Chloe with three slow, firm final thrusts as she desperately gasped for air, her head still spinning from her own orgasm. He leaned forward, sweat dripping from his brow onto Chloe's stomach, and she could hear Avery kiss him again.

Avery collapsed onto the bed next to Chloe, her face radiant with joy, and Ezra leaned down to kiss Chloe, his lips tasting like salt. He then fell to her other side with an exaggerated sigh, making the bed shake as he did. The three lay there, just catching their breath for the longest time. For Chloe, it felt like the whole world had fallen away and it was just the three of them, perfect in that moment. She looked over at Avery, her soft curves looking like a sculpture as she breathed. Her eyes were closed, but she was smiling, her hair a dark pool around her face. She was radiant. Chloe found herself staring at her, basking in the aura of her beauty. After a long moment, Chloe ran her hands over her own body. She felt gorgeous in this moment. She smiled, resting her head back on the mattress. Ezra reached over to take her hand, and she turned to him, meeting the kind and warm gaze from his eyes. Her heart flipped with pure joy as he smiled at her, a quiet chuckle escaping his lips. She laughed back. The three lay wrapped in one another, the only other sound the breeze moving through the leaves of a tree outside their window. Surely, nothing could be better than this.

Chapter 17

Chloe rolled onto her back, watching the shadows from the tree outside her window dance on her ceiling. It was Sunday morning, and she was procrastinating getting out of bed. She sighed to herself, recalling the events of the other night. How soft Avery's skin was, the smells of incense and sweat mixing in that room. It was incredible sex, and Chloe doubted she would ever have better in her life.

She stretched her right hand out over the mattress, and found the sheets cold. Chloe had always slept on the left side of the bed, and even though she was now alone every night, she couldn't bring herself to break the habit and move to the middle. She turned to look at the empty right side of her bed, touching the pillow wistfully. A pillow which had never been slept on. She closed her eyes and imagined Ezra there, smiling at her, speaking the words he had a few nights ago. "Chloe, I love you."

Chloe grimaced as she opened her eyes and sat up, pulling her knees to her chest. *How can he love me?* She thought. *He's never spent more than a few hours at a time with me.* She shook her head, pursing her lips as she thought. Up until now, she had simply been enjoying herself, but those three little words had shocked her back to reality. Polyamory was amazing, and she cared deeply for Ezra and Avery. She certainly didn't want to stop seeing them. They made her so happy. *But what about a year from now?* She thought, glancing at the empty pillow with a sinking feeling in her chest. *Will I still be waking up alone? Will I be happy with that?* In her heart, she knew the answer was no. She definitely needed to have a conversation with Ezra.

Picking up her phone to check the time, she was shocked to realise it was much later than she had thought. Ezra was going to be coming over for a lunch date today, and she wasn't even out of bed. Her hair was a mess, as was her brain, and she sat frozen for a moment before shaking herself into action. She was going to have to talk about what those three little words meant to Ezra. She leapt out of bed and pushed herself into her kitchen, slipping on her slipper as she went. But first, coffee.

Chloe was finishing her now cold cup of coffee, in loose fit pants and a casual shirt, as Ezra's red car pulled into her driveway. She had braided her dyed black hair over one shoulder, and busied herself putting on a bit of makeup to cope with her nervous energy. As she watched from her kitchen window, Ezra stood up out of the car, his blue jeans and neat shirt accentuating his muscles. He pushed his hair back as he closed the door, and Chloe's heart skipped in her chest. For a moment, she considered abandoning the conversation she had spent all morning stressing over. *What if he doesn't want to see me anymore?* She mused, and the thought of it filled her with sadness.

Ezra knocked, having not seen her through the window, and Chloe steadied herself with a deep breath as she set her mug down on the counter, and opened the door. Ezra's face broke into a grin as he saw her, and his baritone voice purred at her "Hey, Chlo."

"Hey," she replied, smiling despite her mind spinning. "Come on in."

"I bought sandwiches," He said, setting a brown paper bag down on the counter. "And coffee. Almond milk and one sugar, right?"

"Right." She said, awkwardly. "Ezra I-"

"I got you chicken and avocado," he continued, digging in the bag. "I know that's your favourite."

"It... it is." She said, softly. *Ah fuck, how am I going to do this.* She paused, biting her lip, as he handed her the sandwich wrapped in paper. He was smiling, his honey eyes glistening. He was so, so attractive. And, although not perfect, he was a really great man. She took the sandwich and smiled. "Thanks," she said, simply.

"Not a problem, Babe." He replied, sitting himself in one of her dining chairs, and unwrapping his meal. "I'm starving."

Chloe nodded, moving herself to join him at the table. She unwrapped her sandwich and took a bite, chewing slowly. She swallowed, and put the sandwich down. "Ezra I-"

His face twisted with concern. "Is there something wrong with the sandwich?"

"No, I-"

"Cos I can take it back." He started to stand.

"No, it's not the sandwich, I-"

"Ah, sorry did they mess up the coffee?"

"No!" She said, exasperated. She put her hand on his arm. "Just sit down. Please. Let me speak."

He looked at her for a second, and she realised she had raised her voice. "Sorry, I didn't mean-"

"It's okay," he said sitting. She levelled him with an annoyed expression.

"Ezra, please stop interrupting me." She said calmly. He nodded.

She sighed, removing her arm from his. Her stomach was in knots, and for a moment she seriously thought about just not saying anything. But she couldn't stay quiet.

"The other night," She started, looking up at Ezra. His face was so kind, genuine, patiently waiting for her. She took a deep breath. "When you said you loved me. I- I'm sorry I can't say it back."

There was a moment where the silence hung in the air. Chloe searched Ezra's face for any glimmer of anger or resentment, but seeing nothing, she continued, the words seeming to fall out of her mouth before she had a chance to think them through really. "But, I really care for you. I do."

He nodded, hands clasped on the table in front of him. She took another deep breath and continued. "I just mean... It's got me thinking. Where is our relationship going?"

He cocked his head, a puzzled look crossing his face. "I don't get what you mean."

"Well," Chloe continued. "You've been dating Avery for six years. Do you see you two getting married eventually?"

"Oh." He said, looking down at his sandwich. He seemed to be genuinely caught off guard. "I guess so. I hadn't really thought about it."

Chloe blinked, a little surprised that in all that time he hadn't considered it at all. "You hadn't?"

"No." He said, looking at her. "Truely I never thought to even ask Avery if that's what she wants." He looked across the room, seeming to turn it in his mind. "Yeah I guess I do see that for us."

"Okay," Chloe said, still a bit stunned that they had never discussed it. "Well, where do I fit in then?"

Ezra looked at her, suddenly very serious. "What do you mean?"

"I mean, am I at your wedding?" The words started tumbling from her mouth now, and she could hear her voice starting to tremble. "Do I get to move in with you? Do I get to meet your parents?" She took a breath, steadying herself. "And when you have kids, what then? Am I Aunty Chloe? Dad's friend Chloe?"

Tears were brimming in her eyes as she looked at him. "Do we have any sort of future, Ezra? Or are we just doomed to fail?"

He looked at her, seemingly stunned. She looked down, embarrassed at her sudden emotion.

"Chloe," he started, reaching his hand towards hers. "I get it, you're worried about Avery getting jealous-"

"No!" She said, looking at him sharply. "That's not it at all. Ezra." She breathed deeply, steadying herself. "I'm afraid you only want me around until you don't have time for me anymore. I'm afraid of getting so caught up in all of this that I lose myself again. I'm afraid-" Her voice caught in her throat and she swallowed it so she could finish. "I'm afraid of being alone."

The air was still, and he looked at her, his deep eyes kind. "Chloe, I can't promise you any of that."

"I know," She said, shaking her head and smiling. "But I also know what I want. And I don't want to wake up alone for the rest of my life."

Ezra nodded, looking down thoughtfully. "I'm not going to leave Avery for you."

"I would never ask you to," Chloe said. Ezra looked up and met her eyes with his.

There was a calm that fell over the two, a moment of understanding. For Chloe, it settled her nerves. She finally felt like they were on the same page. *At least for today,* she thought, with a tinge of sadness. In this moment, she saw the eventual end of their relationship.

"I think," Ezra said, softly. "That I am okay with loving you just for now." He smiled. "I promise to do it to the best of my ability."

Chloe smiled. "I think I can be okay with that."

He leant forward, and kissed her. A deep kiss, full of emotions she had never really felt from him before. Chloe's heart swelled. He pulled back, brushing a strand of hair from her face, seeming to study her every feature. "After all," she continued, smiling. "I could get hit by a bus tomorrow or something."

He smiled, and she could see a tinge of sadness in his eyes. "Please don't do that." He said, and then softer still. "I'm not ready for this chapter to be over just yet."

Chloe sighed, and reached up to his face, his beard course in her fingers. She breathed in his cologne, stared into his honey-coloured eyes. *I'm going to remember this moment.* She thought, resolute.

"Me either." she whispered.

www.ingramcontent.com/pod-product-compliance
Lightning Source LLC
Chambersburg PA
CBHW070519160726
48003CB00004B/1630